Praise for Jhumpa Lahiri's

Roman Stories

"Masterful. . . . Lahiri brilliantly delineates her characters' triumphs and trials." —*Minneapolis Star Tribune*

"[Lahiri's] stories have the beating heart of the city itself, a place of magnificent decay and vibrant, varied life." —*Vogue*

"Each narrative contains deftly drawn vignettes of the entwined lives of Italians and foreigners of different classes, colors, ages, and creeds." — *The Wall Street Journal*

"The fluid transitions between Lahiri's and Portnowitz's translations elevate *Roman Stories* from a grouping of individual tales to a deeply moving whole." —*The New York Times*

"*Roman Stories* simultaneously delivers precision and abundance in lyric short stories that all meditate on how we build our geographies through language. . . . Here, Lahiri builds on her exacting, minimalistic prose that characterizes her English-language work as a means to explore language itself—as she and her characters theorize what it means to belong to a language, to belong to the geography that shapes and makes a language." —*The Brooklyn Rail*

"Supple and elegant. . . . [*Roman Stories*] crackles with indignation as it explores the meaning of home and the cost of exile." —*The Guardian*

"The nine stories in this new collection add up to a vivid portrait of a capital full of splendour. . . . *Roman Stories* is the Indian-American author Jhumpa Lahiri's most substantial work of fiction since she began publishing in Italian in 2018." —*Financial Times*

"A dazzling collection of nine stories originally written in Italian and featuring characters who grapple with vast emotional and social chasms that cleave the lives of families, longtime friends, and immigrants. . . . Throughout, Lahiri's luminous prose captures a side of Rome often ignored. . . . These unembroidered yet potent stories shine." —*Publishers Weekly* (starred review)

"A brilliant return to the short story form by an author of protean accomplishments. . . . Filled with intelligence and sorrow, these sharply drawn glimpses of Roman lives create an impressively unified effect." —*Kirkus Reviews* (starred review)

"Stunning. . . . A finely calibrated collection about insiders and outsiders, natives and foreigners. . . . Rome with its echoing past and mercurial present is a potently evocative setting for Lahiri's exquisitely incisive, richly empathetic, and profoundly resonant stories." —*Booklist* (starred review)

JHUMPA LAHIRI

Roman Stories

Jhumpa Lahiri, a bilingual writer and translator, is the Millicent C. McIntosh Professor of English and Director of Creative Writing at Barnard College, Columbia University. She received the Pulitzer Prize in 2000 for *Interpreter of Maladies* and is also the author of *The Namesake, Unaccustomed Earth*, and *The Lowland*. Since 2015, Lahiri has been writing fiction, essays, and poetry in Italian: *In Altre Parole (In Other Words)*, *Il vestito dei libri (The Clothing of Books)*, *Dove mi trovo* (self-translated as *Whereabouts*), *Il quaderno di Nerina*, and *Racconti romani*. She received the National Humanities Medal from President Barack Obama in 2014, and in 2019 was named Commendatore of the Italian Republic by President Sergio Mattarella. Her most recent book in English, *Translating Myself and Others*, was a finalist for the PEN/Diamonstein-Spielvogel Award for the Art of the Essay.

Roman Stories

Roman Stories

JHUMPA LAHIRI

Translated from the Italian by the author
with Todd Portnowitz

VINTAGE BOOKS
A Division of Penguin Random House LLC
New York

FIRST VINTAGE BOOKS EDITION 2024

English translation copyright © 2023 by Jhumpa Lahiri

All rights reserved. Published in the United States by Vintage Books, a division
of Penguin Random House LLC, New York. Originally published in hardcover in
Italy as *Racconti romani* by Guanda, an imprint of Gruppo editoriale Mauri Spagnol,
Milan, in 2022. Copyright © 2022 by Jhumpa Lahiri. Copyright © 2022 by Ugo Guanda
Editore S.r.l. This translation originally published in hardcover in the United States by
Alfred A. Knopf, a division of Penguin Random House LLC, New York, in 2023.

Vintage and colophon are registered
trademarks of Penguin Random House LLC.

Owing to limitations of space, acknowledgments to reprint previously
published material appear on page 207.

Translated by the author with Todd Portnowitz
Translations of Livy and Ovid by Yelena Baraz and Jhumpa Lahiri

The Library of Congress has cataloged the Knopf edition as follows:
Name: Lahiri, Jhumpa, author, translator.
Title: Roman Stories / Jhumpa Lahiri
Other titles: Racconti romani. English
Description: First United States edition. | New York: Alfred A. Knopf, 2023.
Originally published in hardcover in Italy by Guanda in 2022.
Identifiers: LCCN 2022052100 (print) | LCCN 2022052101 (ebook)
Subjects: LCSH: Lahiri, Jhumpa—Translations into English. | Rome (Italy)—Fiction. |
LCGFT: Short stories.
Classification: LCC PQ5984.L34 R3313 2023 (print) |
LCC PQ5984.L34 (ebook) | DDC 853/.92—dc23
LC record available at https://lccn.loc.gov/2022052100
LC ebook record available at https://lccn.loc.gov/2022052101

Vintage Books Trade Paperback ISBN: 978-0-593-46990-3
eBook ISBN: 978-0-593-53633-9

Book design by Cassandra J. Pappas

vintagebooks.com

Printed in the United States of America
10 9 8 7 6 5 4 3 2 1

For Noor, Octavio, and Alberto:

ten years later

Crescebat interim urbs munitionibus alia atque alia appetendo loca, cum in spem magis futurae multitudinis quam ad id quod tum hominum erat munirent.

Meanwhile the city was growing this way and that, building walls and striving to gain new ground; they built walls hoping for a population that would be greater, one day, than the people there at the time.

—Livy, *Ab urbe condita,* I, 8

nondum tamen invia Iani
ora patentis erant, neque iter praecluserat unda

But the gaping gates of Janus were still unblocked; the current hadn't barred the way.

—Ovid, *Metamorphoses,* XIV, 789–90

Contents

Part I

The Boundary

EVERY SATURDAY, a new family comes to stay. Some arrive early in the morning, from afar, ready to begin their vacation. Others don't turn up until sunset, in bad moods, maybe having lost their way. It's easy to get lost in these hills; the roads are poorly signposted.

Today, after they introduce themselves, I show them around. My mother used to do the welcoming. But she's spending the summer in a nearby town, helping out an elderly gentleman who's also on vacation, so I have to do it.

As usual, there are four of them: mother, father, two daughters. They follow me, wide-eyed, happy to stretch their legs.

We stop for a moment on the shaded patio that looks out over the lawn, under a thatched roof that filters the light. There are two armchairs and a sofa, covered with white fabric, lounge chairs for sunbathing, and a wooden table big enough for ten people.

I open the sliding glass door and show them inside: the cozy living room with two comfortable sofas in front of the fireplace, the well-stocked kitchen, two bedrooms.

While the father unloads the car and the girls, who are probably around seven and nine, disappear into their room, shutting the door behind them, I tell the mother where to find extra towels, and woolen blankets, in case it gets cold at night.

I show her where the mouse poison is hidden. Kill the flies before going to bed, I suggest, otherwise they start buzzing at dawn and become a nuisance. I explain how to get to the supermarket, how to use the washing machine behind the house, and where to hang the laundry, just on the other side of my father's garden.

Guests are free to pick lettuce and tomatoes, I add. There were lots of tomatoes this year, but most of them spoiled in the July rain.

· 2 ·

I pretend not to watch them, to be discreet. I do the housework and water the garden, but I can't help noticing how happy and excited they are. I hear the girls' voices as they run across the lawn, I learn their names. Since the guests usually leave the sliding door open, I overhear what the parents say to each other as they settle into the house, as they unpack their suitcases and decide what to have for lunch.

The cottage where my family lives is a few yards away, behind a tall hedge that forms a kind of screen. For years, our house was just a room that served as both kitchen and bedroom for the three of us. Then, two years ago, when I turned thirteen, my mother started working for the elderly gentleman, and, after saving up enough money, my parents asked the man who owns the property if they could add a small room for me—where stubby lizards slip through cracks between the wall and ceiling.

My father is the caretaker. He looks after the big house, chops wood, works the fields and the vineyard. He looks after the horses, which the owner loves with a passion.

The owner lives abroad, but he's not a foreigner like us. He comes every now and then, on his own. He doesn't have a family. During the days he goes horseback riding; in the evenings he reads in front of the fireplace. Then he goes away again.

Not many people rent his house other than in summer. The winters here are biting, and in the spring there's lots of rain. In the mornings, from September to June, my father drives me to school, where I feel out of place. I don't mix easily with others; I don't look like anyone else.

The girls in this family resemble each other. You can tell right away that they're sisters. They've already put on matching bathing suits to go to the beach later on. The beach is about fifteen miles from here. The mother looks like a girl, too. She's small and thin, she wears her long hair loose. Her shoulders are delicate. She walks barefoot on the grass even though the father tells her not to, saying (and he's right) that there might be porcupines, hornets, snakes.

· 3 ·

After just a few hours, it's as if they'd always lived here. The things they've brought for a week in the country are scattered all over the place: books, magazines, a laptop computer, dolls, hoodies, colored pencils, pads of paper, flip-flops, sunscreen. At lunch I hear forks striking plates. I notice each time one of them sets a glass down on the table. I detect the calm thread of their conversation, the sound and smell of the coffeepot, smoke from a cigarette.

After lunch, the father asks one of the girls to bring him his glasses. For a long time, he studies a road map. He lists small towns to visit nearby, archaeological sites, ruins. The mother isn't interested. She says this is her only week of the year without appointments and obligations.

Later on, the father heads off to the sea with his daughters. He asks me, as they're leaving, how long it takes to get there, which of the beaches is nicest. He asks me about the weather forecast for the week, and I tell him there's a heat wave coming.

The mother stays home. She's put on her bathing suit anyway, to get some sun.

She stretches out on one of the lounge chairs. I assume she's going to take a nap, but when I go to hang up the wash I see her writing something. She writes by hand, in a little notebook resting on her thighs.

Now and then she lifts her head and looks intently at the landscape that surrounds us. She stares at the various greens of the lawn, the hills, the woods in the distance. The glaring blue of the sky, the yellow hay. The bleached fence, and the low stone wall that marks the property line. She looks at all the things I look at every day. But I wonder what else she sees in them.

· 4 ·

When the sun starts to set, they put on sweaters and long pants to shield themselves from mosquitoes. The father and the girls have wet hair from the hot showers they took after the beach.

The girls tell their mother about their trip: the burning sand, the slightly murky water, the gentle, disappointing waves. The whole family goes for a short walk. They go to look at the horses, the donkeys, a wild boar kept in a pen behind the stables. They go to see the flock of sheep that passes in front of the house every day around this time, that blocks the cars on the dusty road for a few minutes.

The father keeps taking pictures with his cell phone. He shows the girls the small plum trees, the fig trees, the olives. He says fruit picked straight from the tree has a different flavor. It tastes like the sun, the countryside.

The parents open a bottle of wine on the patio. They try some cheese, the local honey. They admire the blazing landscape and marvel at the huge, glowing clouds, the color of pomegranates in October.

Evening falls. They hear frogs, crickets, rustling wind. In spite of the breeze, they decide to eat outside, to take advantage of the lingering light.

My father and I eat inside, in silence. He doesn't look up when he eats. With my mother away, there's no conversation during dinner. She's the one who talks at meals.

My mother can't stand this place, this town. Like my father, she comes from much farther away than anyone who vacations here. She hates living out in the country, in the middle of nowhere. She says the people around here aren't nice, that they're closed off.

I don't miss her complaining. I don't like listening to her, even though she's probably right. Sometimes, when she complains too much, my father sleeps in the car instead of in bed with her.

After dinner, the girls wander around the lawn chasing fireflies. They play with their flashlights. The parents sit on the patio contemplating the starry sky, the intense darkness.

The mother sips hot water with lemon, the father a little grappa. They say that being here is all they need, that even the air is different, that it cleanses. How lovely, they say, being together like this, away from everyone.

· 5 ·

First thing in the morning, I go to the chicken coop to gather eggs. They're warm and pale, filthy. I put a few in a bowl and bring them to the guests for breakfast. Normally there's no one around and I just leave them on the patio table. But then I notice, through the sliding door, that the girls are already awake. I see bags of cookies on the sofa, crumbs, a cereal box overturned on the coffee table.

The girls are trying to swat the flies that buzz around the house in the morning. The older one is holding the flyswatter. The little sister, frustrated, complains that she's still waiting for her turn. She says she wants to swat them, too.

I put down the eggs and go back to our house. Then I knock on their door and lend the girls our flyswatter; that way they're both happy. I don't remind them that it's better to kill the flies before you go to bed. It's clear that they're having fun while the parents, in spite of the annoying flies and the girls' racket, continue sleeping.

· 6 ·

After two days, a predictable routine sets in. In the late morning, the father goes to the café in town, to buy milk and the paper, to get a second coffee. He pops over to the supermarket if need be. When he gets back, he goes running in the hills despite the humidity. One morning he comes home rattled, after a sheepdog blocked the path and growled at him, even though nothing happened in the end.

The mother does what I do: she sweeps the floor, cooks, washes dishes. At least once a day she hangs up the laundry. Our clothes mingle and dry on the same line. She tells her husband, clasping the laundry basket in her arms, how happy this makes her. Since they live in the city, in a crowded apartment, she can never hang their clothes out in the open like this.

After lunch, the father takes the girls to the beach and the mother stays home alone. She stretches out and smokes a cigarette, writing in her notebook with an air of concentration.

One day, back from the beach, the girls run around for hours trying to catch the crickets that leap through the grass. They snatch them up. They put a few in a jar with little pieces of tomato stolen from their parents' salads. They turn them into pets, even give them names. The next day the crickets die, suffocated in the jar, and the girls cry. They bury them under one of the plum trees and put some wildflowers on top.

Another day, the father discovers that one of the flip-flops he'd left outside is missing. I tell him a fox probably took it; there's been one prowling around. I tell my father, who knows the habits and hideouts of all the animals around here, and he manages to find the shoe, along with a ball and a shopping bag abandoned by the previous family.

I realize how much the guests like this rural, unchanging landscape, how much they appreciate every detail, how these things help them think, rest, dream. When the girls pick black-berries, staining the pretty dresses they're wearing, the mother doesn't get mad at them. Instead she laughs. She asks the father to take a picture, and then throws the dresses in the wash.

At the same time I wonder what they know about the lone-liness here. About the identical days in our dilapidated cottage. The nights when the wind blows so hard the earth seems to shake, or when the sound of rain keeps me awake. The months we live alone among the hills, the horses, the insects, the birds that pass over the fields. What would they make of the harsh quiet that reigns here all winter?

· 7 ·

On the last night, other cars arrive. Friends of the parents, invited along with their children, who run around the meadow. A couple of them report that the traffic was light coming in from the city. The adults take a look around the house, walk in the garden at sunset. The table on the patio is already set.

I hear everything as they eat. The laughter and chatter are louder tonight. The family relates all their mishaps in the country: the tomato-eating crickets and their funeral under the plum tree, the sheepdog, the fox that carried off the flip-flop. The mother says that being in touch with nature like this has been good for the girls.

At a certain point a cake comes out, with candles, and I realize it's the father's birthday. He's turning forty-five. Everyone sings and they slice the cake.

My father and I finish up some overripe grapes. I'm about to clear the table when I hear a knock at the door. I see the girls, hesitant, out of breath. They give me a plate with two slices of cake on it: one for me and one for my father. They dash off before I can say thanks.

We eat the cake while the guests talk about politics, trips, life in the city. Someone asks the mother where she got the cake, and she tells them that one of the guests picked it up; the guest chimes in with the name of the bakery, the piazza it's in.

My father lays down his fork and lowers his head. His eyes are agitated when he looks at me. He gets up abruptly and then steps out to smoke a cigarette, unobserved.

· 8 ·

We used to live in the city, too. My father sold flowers in that very piazza. My mother used to help.

They spent their days next to each other in a small but pleasant stand, arranging bouquets that people took home to decorate their tables and terraces. New to this country, they learned the names of the flowers: rose, sunflower, carnation, daisy. They kept them, their stems submerged, in a row of buckets.

One night three men showed up. My father was alone; my mother, pregnant with me at the time, was at home, because he didn't want her to work at night. It was late. The other stores around the piazza were closed, and my father was about to lower his metal shutters.

One of the men asked him to open up again, saying that he was on his way to see his girlfriend. He wanted a nice bouquet. My father agreed that he'd make him one, even though the men were rude, a little drunk.

When my father held up the bouquet the man said that it was skimpy and asked him to make it bigger. My father added more flowers, an excessive number, until the man was satisfied. He wrapped paper around the bouquet, then he bound it up with colored ribbon, tying a bow. He told him the price.

The man pulled some money out of his wallet. It wasn't enough. And when my father refused to hand over the bouquet the man told him that he was an idiot, that he didn't even know how to put together a nice bouquet for a beautiful girl. Then, together with the others, he started beating my father until his mouth filled with blood, until his front teeth were shattered.

My father yelled, but at that hour no one heard. They said, Go back to wherever you came from. They took the bouquet and left him like that on the ground.

My father went to the emergency room. He couldn't eat solid foods for a year. After I was born, when he saw me for the first time, he couldn't say a word.

Ever since, he's struggled to speak. He garbles his words, as if he were an old man. He's ashamed to smile, because of his missing teeth. My mother and I understand him, but others don't. They think, since he's a foreigner, that he doesn't speak the language. Sometimes they even think he's mute.

When the pears and red apples that grow in the garden are ripe, we cut them into thin slices, almost transparent, so that he can savor them.

One of his compatriots told him about this job, in this secluded place. He wasn't familiar with the countryside: he'd always lived in cities.

He can live and work here without opening his mouth. He's not afraid of being attacked. He prefers to live among the animals, cultivating the land. He's gotten used to this untamed place that protects him.

When he talks to me, as he drives me to school, he always says the same thing: that he couldn't make anything of his life. All he wants me to do is study and finish school, go to college, and then go far away from them.

· 9 ·

The next day, late in the morning, the father starts to load the car. I see four people, tanned, even more closely knit. They don't want to leave. At breakfast they say that they'd like to come back next year. Nearly all the guests say the same thing when they go. A few faithfully return, but for most of them once is enough.

Before heading out, the mother shows me the stuff in the fridge that they don't want to take back to the city. She tells me that she's grown quite fond of this house, that she already misses it. Maybe, when she's feeling stressed, or overwhelmed by work, she'll think of this place: the clean air, the hills, the clouds blazing at sunset.

I wish the family safe travels and say goodbye. I stand there waiting until the car's out of sight. Then I start to prepare the house for the new family that's scheduled to arrive. I make the beds. I tidy the room the girls turned upside down. I sweep the flies they swatted.

They've forgotten, or left on purpose, a few things they don't need, things I hold on to. Pictures the girls drew, shells they picked up at the beach, the last drops of a scented shower gel. Shopping lists in the faint, small script that the mother used, on other sheets of paper, to write all about us.

The Reentry

ON A SUNNY DAY in September, two women meet on the Ponte Sisto and embrace. It's been a year since they've seen each other. They step over the low rusty chain that blocks traffic on the bridge. Lovers affix padlocks to the links; distracted pedestrians tend to trip over them. It's past two in the afternoon, and both women are hungry.

One of them, raised close to the bridge, is in mourning. Her father died a few weeks before, and she's also grieving for her dying marriage. She's a thin, short woman with blond hair pulled back, big green eyes, and an earlobe studded with diamonds and small gold hoops.

The other woman is a university professor. She has darker hair and darker skin and she's taller than her friend. At the moment, she's also happier. She's just celebrated her birthday at the sea, so she's tanned and feels rejuvenated. She's been meaning to meet up with her friend who's going through a hard time, who's facing a separation and the loss of her father.

"When did you get back?" she asks, linking elbows with the woman in mourning as they walk.

"About ten days ago. What about you?"

"Day before yesterday."

The two women, who both have children around the same age, met one another some years ago in the playground at Piazza San Cosimato. When they both lived in Rome they would often have lunch together in a trattoria and talk for hours.

But for the past two years the woman in mourning, the one who's returned for her father's funeral, has been living in another city, in a country not far from Italy. She went to live there with her two children but without her husband, who had to stay on in Rome for his job, though back then, things between them were still relatively smooth. The woman was forty-six and wanted a change of scenery; she was tired of the run-down city she'd been born in.

The professor, too, has recently returned to Rome, not to face a loss but to enjoy a year on sabbatical with her family. She knows the city well and loves it. She visits often to conduct research or to attend conferences, either on her own or with her family, at times for lengthy stays. Ancient Roman history is her field.

Today the woman in mourning has booked a table at a trattoria she's particularly fond of. It's one of the few, she says, that's held out—stubbornly and marvelously—against the flow of time. "It'll be a chance to show you something new," she says. "Even though my city is your city by now."

In order to reach the trattoria they walk past the elegant palazzo where the parents of the woman in mourning lived for the greater part of the year. "It's so strange to think that he'll never go back there," she says now, referring to her father. He was a journalist who spoke five languages and traveled the world. In the summers her parents would decamp to the mountains, where it was cooler. Her father, who was over ninety, had died in the same bed in the mountains in which he'd been born. The city house was always empty in the summers, but now it held a different sort of emptiness.

The woman in mourning tells her friend that, earlier in the day, she'd gone in quickly to fetch a few things and that she'd been surrounded, as a result, by paintings, books, and other objects belonging to her father. Needless to say, it had shaken her.

"Were you with him when he passed away?" the professor asks.

"I was on the plane, I didn't make it in time."

The trattoria is on a street without a sidewalk in a warren-like neighborhood that's always crowded. It's the same part of the city where, years ago, the professor had rented an apartment for the summer, on the very same street where the woman in mourning had grown up. The two women liked to remark on this coincidence: the fact that they'd both lived on the same street in different stages of life, under different circumstances.

When they reach the trattoria they nearly walk by it; the façade is discreet to the point of anonymity. It looks nothing like the other trattorie nearby, always thronged with tourists. For example, it looks nothing like the trattoria that had so warmly welcomed the professor and her family every evening that first summer. That one had bottles of wine in the window and tattered white umbrellas over the tables outside, on a sloping piazza, arranged against a peeling wall. Now and then the two brothers who ran the place would set a big bottle of Averna on the table before bringing the bill.

The trattoria they enter today looks restrained by comparison, with two glass doors that correspond to two different buildings. One building is covered in bricks and the other has a smooth façade painted in large squares of pink and pale orange. One of the two doors, which is closed, flanks the entrance. The other serves as a window. They're both made of frosted glass so that no one walking by can see inside. The two women have to ring a bell to be admitted, and since the entrance is set off at an angle one can barely glimpse the interior from the street.

Once inside, the woman in mourning greets the padrona: a thickset woman with thin-framed glasses and short white hair. Then she recognizes and greets a man sitting at a table in the corner with a boy who looks to be about six years old. From their affectionate exchange the professor understands that he's an old friend, and that he, too, grew up a stone's throw from this trattoria.

"Sorry to sit with my back to you," the woman in mourning says to the man as she takes her seat.

"Let me sit there," her friend suggests, and so they switch places and rest their purses on the empty chair between them.

The trattoria is shaped like an L. The white walls, the black molding, and the pale marble wainscoting make it feel like the spare, paradoxically immaculate interior of a butcher shop. The woman in mourning is facing her old friend sitting in the corner and the professor is facing a table of men, all well dressed, who probably work in the same office. It's impossible to see what's behind the corner.

On the table there's a menu in a transparent plastic sleeve: a white sheet of paper with a typewritten list of all the dishes. It sits there untouched; neither of the women bothers to look at it.

The padrona, who is also the waitress and the cook, tells them what there is to eat. She has burly arms and wears an apron over a white cotton shirt with short sleeves. The woman in mourning asks for vegetables to start, and then a plate of pasta.

"And what shall we bring out for *la moretta*?" the padrona asks briskly, without looking directly at the professor.

After a moment she replies, "I'll have the same." But she feels nettled, as if the nearly weightless but prickly legs of an insect were to rest briefly on the back of her hand.

"What exactly does that mean, when people say *la moretta*?" the professor asks.

"Oh, it's nothing, people use it to describe anyone with dark hair," says the woman in mourning, aware that her friend looks vaguely upset.

Now that they're seated the professor notices that her friend looks exhausted.

"Are you sleeping?"

"Not much."

"Eating?"

"I will today. The food here is always good."

At that very moment the padrona brings out a bottle of water and a basket with just two slices of bread. Then she brings them some boiled greens, dark and shiny.

"Here you go, sweetheart," she says to the woman in mourning. And to the other woman: "And the same for the pretty lady."

The new epithet, delivered offhandedly, the tone a bit harsh, also troubles the professor.

"How are the kids coping through all this?" she asks her grieving friend. Each of them has one boy and one girl.

"They've figured it out by now. I left them in the mountains with my mother. Here, I'll show you." The professor, too, searches for her cell phone in her purse.

"Your daughter looks just like you," the woman in mourning observes.

"Yours, on the other hand, looks like her father," her friend says. Then she asks, gently: "Is he still with that colleague of his?"

"So I gather. It is what it is."

"How did you find out?"

"I think I already knew, or at least I sensed something. Maybe that's why I wanted to leave Rome. Because something already felt off-kilter."

"So you did the right thing."

"Back then I didn't want to face it. I thought I'd do what you did—go discover a new place with my children. But that move only speeded up a dissolving marriage."

The woman in mourning says she's already spoken to a lawyer, but given that she now lives in another city with her children, it's a complicated situation.

She interrupts herself to say goodbye to her old friend, who's finished his lunch.

"Isn't the food here delicious?" she asks the boy. "Imagine,

I used to come here when I was your age. Just like you, for lunch, with my father."

The boy, timid, looks back at her wide-eyed without saying anything.

At that moment the padrona returns with the pasta.

"You're talking too much, you haven't finished your vegetables," she says, kindly scolding the woman in mourning.

This time there's no epithet for the professor.

The pasta, piping hot, is bland but satisfying.

As they're eating, the cell phone of the woman in mourning starts ringing.

"I'm at lunch with a friend," she says, then asks the person who's called to pass by the trattoria. She explains that it's a neighbor of her parents. He needs to give her the mail that's been piling up at their apartment, including several telegrams that have arrived since her father's death.

A few minutes later, the neighbor arrives with a big black envelope. He kisses the woman in mourning and gives the professor a firm handshake.

"Have a seat," the woman in mourning says. "Would you like a coffee?"

"No, thanks. Here's the mail."

They talk about her father, and the woman in mourning sums up his last days, his deathbed wishes, the funeral.

"He went just as he would have wished," she says sadly, without shedding a tear.

"He was an exceptional man," the neighbor says. "I always admired his thirst for travel, for other worlds. We'll miss him."

He says goodbye to the women and leaves. The men at the

nearby table are also standing up to go. A few glance at the professor, curious.

"And you, are you happy to be back in this city?" the woman in mourning asks her friend.

"Returning to Rome is always wonderful, and never the same," she replies. Then she adds: "It's the only place where I really feel at home."

As she says this, however, she fears that her relationship with the city is actually quite tenuous. In the end, she has no personal link to the history she studies, nor will she ever experience the comfort of having lunch in a trusted restaurant that forms part of her family's history, that holds within it memories of countless lunches between father and daughter, a space that soothes her friend even after such an immense loss.

Someone has turned off a few lights, so that the interior of the trattoria is darker now, as if a rainstorm is about to pass through.

"Shall we leave?" the woman in mourning suggests.

"Let's go."

"Let me run to the bathroom."

"Okay, I'll go after you."

Alone at the table, the professor studies the tablecloth, the design of the trattoria's logo, the neglected menu. She wonders if her family would enjoy the place. But then she asks herself if the padrona would call her daughter, who resembles her, a *moretta*. Regardless, she thinks that it's good to live in a place that's both familiar and full of secrets, with discoveries that reveal themselves only slowly and by chance.

"It's like we're in their home," the woman in mourning says, amused, when she returns to the table.

The professor gets up to find the bathroom. Turning the corner, she realizes that, in addition to the padrona, there's another woman, slightly younger, at the cash register, with black hair that looks dyed, and that there is also a little girl, maybe six or seven, who's been silent all this time. The two women might be sisters, and the girl one of their granddaughters. They keep a distracted eye on the girl, who seems idle in that cramped space.

"Is this the bathroom?" the professor asks, pointing to a door with nothing written on it.

The younger of the two women confirms, a bit drily, that it is.

Inside the bathroom, the professor reflects on her friend's observation—that it's like being in someone's home. It's just an ordinary bathroom in a trattoria. And yet she feels ill at ease and in the way.

When she steps out, she sees the little girl seated on the floor with her legs splayed. As a result, she can't get by. She waits a few seconds for the girl to move. But the girl just sits there, frozen. The padrona and the woman at the register don't tell her to get up. They don't say anything. And so the professor asks the girl:

"May I?"

The girl neither replies nor reacts, behaving as if she hasn't heard. At this point the professor cautiously steps over one of the girl's bare legs so that she can go back to the table.

As soon as she's crossed the small barrier of flesh and blood she hears the girl whisper some sort of complaint, but she can't quite make out the words. She makes sense of it from the padrona's reply:

"You're the one who needs to move aside for her."

Though she says this, it's in that same restrained, offhanded way, so that the professor feels ill at ease again.

"Let's ask for the check," the woman in mourning says when she sees her friend.

They leave the table and proceed to pay. The little girl is in the same spot, her stiff legs still splayed.

When the woman in mourning approaches, she immediately moves one of her legs to let her pass.

But when the professor appears, the girl blocks her way again.

Then she says to the two who appear to be sisters, pointing to the woman in mourning, who stands in front, "She's the nice one."

No one says anything.

The girl insists, "She's nicer than the other one."

The padrona replies, calmly: "All women are nice, and you're a little brat."

"But she's the nice one," the girl repeats, agitated. "I don't like the other one."

"You're right, my friend is very nice," the professor says lightly, even as she feels her spirits sink. Then, hoping to break up the increasingly rigid atmosphere with some humor, she adds, "And why is it that you don't like me?"

But the child, like the padrona, refuses to speak directly to the professor, just as she refused to move her leg. Instead she says, to the padrona and to the woman at the cash register: "I don't like the other one. She's bad, very bad."

This snuffs out the professor's feeble attempt to win her over.

The woman in mourning, who has her back to the girl, is absorbed by the check and doesn't pay attention. The padrona and the woman at the cash register are still mute. No one tells the girl to be quiet or to apologize.

The woman in mourning shows her friend the check. Her friend pulls out some money, quietly, mechanically, from her wallet. It's a sum that can't be split evenly, and the change is also uneven, and the professor ends up paying slightly more, the woman in mourning slightly less.

"I owe you five," says the woman in mourning.

"Don't worry, you'll get it next time," her friend replies.

The little girl keeps saying that the woman in mourning is nice and that the professor is bad. She repeats it as if it were some sort of inane, sinister nursery rhyme until finally the woman at the cash register snaps: "Now get up, come on, I'm taking you back to your mother."

"Thank you, *arrivederci*," the woman in mourning says to the woman at the cash register.

"Goodbye, *Dottoressa*," she replies.

"Say hello to your mother," the padrona adds.

"Can you explain what just happened in there?" the professor asks, once they're outside the trattoria. She's sweating, but not from the heat.

"Let it go, that little girl was rude."

"But she was more than that. She was full of rage."

"Forget about it. I'm sorry."

"I'm sorry, too. You wanted to take me there, but I'll never go back again."

"No, you won't."

They cross the bridge together, stepping over the first chain weighted down with forgotten promises, then the second. They continue to replay the episode in the trattoria: the little girl's unpunished conviction and the stubborn silence of both women. On the other side of the bridge, they hug each other.

"Ciao, *ciccia*. We'll talk soon."

"Goodbye, my dear, you be well."

They let go, but the levity of their old goodbyes is missing.

After a few minutes, the professor reaches Piazza San Cosimato and rests on a dirty, boiling-hot bench. Her lunch sits in her stomach like a rock. She doesn't just feel bad and embittered; she's humiliated, gripped by a sadness she can't control.

The woman in mourning, meanwhile, crosses the river and sits on another bench in the shade, where she sorts through her parents' mail and reads some postcards written to her dead father, consoling herself with the condolences of loved ones, sent from near and far.

P's Parties

· 1 ·

I SHOULD NOTE straightaway that P's parties took place every year at her house, on a Saturday or Sunday afternoon, during the mild winters we typically enjoy in this city.

Unlike the slog of other winter holidays spent with family, always arduous, P's birthday, at the beginning of the new year, was an unpredictable gathering, languorous and light. I looked forward to the commotion of the crowded house, the pots of water on the verge of boiling, the smartly dressed wives always ready to lend a hand in the kitchen. I waited for the first few glasses of prosecco before lunch to go to my head, sampled the various appetizers. Then I liked to join the other adults out on the patio for a little fresh air, to smoke a cigarette and comment on the soccer game the kids played without interruption in the yard.

The atmosphere at P's party was warm but impersonal, owing to the number of people invited, who knew one another either too well or not at all. You'd encounter two distinct groups, like two opposing currents that crisscross in the ocean, forming a perfectly symmetrical shape, only to cancel each other out a moment later. On one side there were those like me and my wife, old friends of P and her husband who came every year, and on the other our counterparts: foreigners who'd show up for a few years, or sometimes just once.

They came from different countries, for work or for love, for a change of scenery, or for some other mysterious reason. They were a nomadic population that piqued my interest— prototypes, perhaps, for one of my future stories, the kind of people I'd have the chance to meet and casually observe only at P's house. In no time at all they'd manage to visit nearly all parts of our country, tackling the smaller towns on the week- ends, skiing our mountains in February, and swimming in our crystalline seas in July. They'd pick up a decent smattering of our language, adapt to the food, forgive the daily chaos. Over- night they'd become minor experts in the historical events we'd memorized as kids and had all but forgotten—which emperor succeeded which, what they accomplished. They had a strategic relationship with this city without ever fully being a part of it, knowing that sooner or later their trip would end and one day they'd be gone.

They were so different from the group I belonged to: those of us born and raised in Rome, who bemoaned the city's alarming decline but could never leave it behind. The type of people for whom just moving to a new neighborhood in their thirties—going to a new pharmacy, buying the newspaper from a different newsstand, finding a table at a different coffee bar—was the equivalent of departure, displacement, complete rupture.

· 2 ·

P was an old friend of my wife's. They'd known each other for many years, before we started dating, having grown up on the same block lined with grand palazzi. As kids they played together until dark; they went to the same elementary school and then the same challenging high school; they wandered off to buy contraband cigarettes from a shady guy behind a piazza that was quiet in those days. They went to the same university and, after graduating, rented a fifth-floor apartment in the thick of the city center. In the summers they traveled together to other countries—experiences they still loved to talk about. Then matters of the heart intervened: my wife met me at a New Year's Eve party, while P married a staid but friendly lawyer, a man of average height, good looking but slightly cross-eyed, and became a mother of four—three boys in quick succession, and then, like a simple but welcome dessert after a three-course meal, a girl.

Not long before the girl was born, P had a brush with death. A renowned doctor, always among those invited to the party, ended up saving her life with a tricky surgery. From then on, this yearly gathering became a constant: this sunny afternoon around her birthday, this merry, lavish lunch that brought together a wide range of people. P liked to fill the house and churn her friends together—relatives, neighbors, parents of her children's classmates. She liked to throw open the door at least fifty times, offering something to eat, playing host, exchanging a few words with everyone.

It was thanks to my wife, then, that I went to that house once a year, a somewhat secluded house on the city's outskirts.

To get there, you took a curved, picturesque road, lined with cypresses and tumbling ivy. A road that swept you away, an urban road that ferried you toward the sea and put the frenzied city far behind. At a certain point there was a sharp right turn; you had to keep an eye out, it was easy to miss. After that it became a sort of residential labyrinth, with narrow, shaded, unpaved streets. You couldn't see the houses, just tall gates and the house numbers etched in stone.

P's house, where she lived with her children, her husband, and their two dogs, was at one end of this labyrinth. A spacious home, recently constructed, airy, with large, open rooms and plenty of space for a hundred-plus people to move about. At first glance—the house sat on a vast lawn, with no other structure in sight—it resembled a big, white, square-shaped rock jutting out of a green sea. In the distance you could glimpse the faint outline of the city where my wife and I and nearly all the other guests lived. It had a certain effect on me, coming to that house from our pleasant but compact apartment, where every book, every spoon, every shirt had its proper place, where I knew every shelf and hinge, and seating ten at the dinner table was a squeeze. An apartment whose windows looked out only onto other apartments, other windows, other lives like ours.

My memories of the past five or so of those parties had blurred together. Each year was different, and each year, for the most part, was the same. I made the same small talk I'd forget a minute later, I practiced my two rusty but still passable foreign languages, which I'd always brush up on a bit. I indulged, perhaps a little too much, in the same delicacies arrayed on the buffet table, circling back for more, with no regard for the extra kilos I'd put on and fret over after all those holiday meals. I said hello to friends and kissed the cheeks of women in their forties and fifties who staunchly refused to play the role of *signora*. I absorbed the scent of their expensive perfumes, made brief contact with the warm skin of their shoulders, admired the elegant, form-fitting dresses they could still get away with at their age, at our age. At P's parties I felt embraced, cared for, and at the same time blissfully ignored, free. We were detached from our flawed, finely tuned lives, from our frustrations. I could sense time lengthening and the suspension, at least for a few hours, of all responsibility.

I wouldn't have been able to distinguish one party from the next, the incidents, the particulars, until one year when something out of the ordinary occurred, an ultimately banal disruption that remains a caesura in my life.

· 3 ·

That year, I remember everything very precisely. I remember, for example, that there was more traffic than usual, which meant that we got there an hour late. It didn't matter, at P's it was always buffet-style. I remember that my wife was telling me a story, talking ceaselessly as I drove, and that I was tuning her out. In fact, her slightly hoarse voice and her tendency to be long-winded were getting on my nerves. She managed an art gallery. I'd have preferred to drive that scenic stretch of road in silence, but she went on about clients and promising young painters. Before getting out of the car, she changed her shoes, trading her comfortable flats for a fancier pair with heels, partly to gain an extra inch or two and become just a touch taller than me.

Because P always invited all her children's friends, the first thing we saw, walking up to the house, was a swarm of younger and older kids playing out in the yard, in the sun. Their coats were strewn on the grass, like towels left on the beach while everyone goes for a swim. The grade schoolers and teenagers ran around, in good spirits, sweating, and P's pair of dogs were barking and chasing after them.

I thought of our own boy with a pang of nostalgia, the one child my wife and I had brought into this world. Just the other day he'd have come with us, and he, too, would have played in the yard without his coat. But now he was a grown man, a college graduate, a few months into his new life abroad, pursuing further studies at a foreign university.

My wife didn't mourn his absence—if anything, she was eager for him to become more and more independent. According to her, the fact that he was getting by on his own for the most part, and now had a woman in his life, and was far from us, was a much deserved and happy ending to our long and exhausting road as parents. It meant that we'd done a good job, and this was a milestone worth celebrating. I found her lack of worry astonishing: she who'd hovered over our son his whole life, who'd taken such exacting care of his every meal, every soccer game, every test, every report card. But then I realized that she was always looking ahead, very rarely behind, which was why she now had her sights on his career, his love life, his future children—in short, his complete separation from us. While, for me, not seeing him every day, not hearing his voice around the house, or even his mediocre violin playing, not knowing what he was up to, not adding his favorite juice to the grocery cart—it all came as a blow. I was proud of him, yes, I was excited about his prospects, but I still had a hole in my heart.

We rang the bell even though the door was ajar. We kissed cheeks with P and her husband, who were there to greet us at the entrance as always. P was in fine form, radiant, wearing a printed dress from the seventies that had belonged to her mother, with a leather belt to accentuate her waist. We'd come bearing a few gifts: a scented candle, body cream, a new novel that everyone was talking about. After we chatted a minute, the doorbell rang again and we were ushered down the hall. We took off our coats and threw them on the couch, atop an already precarious, promiscuous mound of fabric. It was warm in the house, but my wife, who is sensitive to cold and was wearing a sleeveless dress, decided to keep her pearl-gray wool shawl around her shoulders.

We found our way to the bar and picked up two glasses of prosecco. We made a toast, locking eyes for a moment. Then, with no hard feelings, for the rest of the afternoon my wife and I moved through the party in separate circles, paying each other no mind.

I began wandering about the house as if it were a favorite haunt, a place I knew fairly well but always partially, encountering one friend after another. It was only in this house, at this party, that we—mired in our responsibilities, in the personal and professional obligations that devour us, that define us—found the calm and the time to catch up. We ate, shared our news, chatted aimlessly.

All the while I was paying close attention to that other

group: my potential fictional characters, the foreigners with whom I'd exchange just a few words, or more glances than words, really. I was intrigued by their point of view. They fascinated me precisely because, even though we were crammed into the same house, celebrating the same mutual friend, partaking in the same collective ritual, we remained two species, distinct and unmistakable. Eventually they'd drift off into their relaxed and secluded conversations, and we into ours. They seemed proud of their decision to uproot their lives, to acquire, in middle age, new points of reference. They evoked a world beyond my horizons, the risky steps I'd never taken: a world that had perhaps snatched my son away for good.

After making the rounds inside, I went out onto the patio. I stole a cigarette, one of the few I allow myself on occasion when unwinding away from home, and I joined the others watching the mix of younger and older kids still playing soccer, making a racket in the yard. The trees scattered around the lawn were turning gold in the light. At first, we were all men. Then P joined our conversation for a minute, to make sure we had everything we needed, something to drink, something to eat. She treated each of us like a lifelong friend, even though she hardly knew most of her guests.

"You've got a fantastic lawn. It would be nice to put a pool back here," one of the men said to her.

"It's not worth it. Every summer we spend two months at the sea," P replied.

"Oh, where?"

"A tiny island, in the middle of nowhere, rather remote. You have to take a boat to buy groceries."

"You don't mind?"

"Not at all. It's the inconvenience I crave. I've been going there since I was a little girl."

"How wonderful."

"In August the entire island smells of rosemary. There's a small lighthouse, a pool in the middle, the sea all around, and that's about it," P said.

I'd never been to that island, but I'd heard about it from my wife, who used to go there for a week or so every summer as a guest of P's family. Then one year—my wife told me— a man, a great swimmer who did twenty laps in the pool twice a day, died right there in the water, while racing a friend, struck by a heart attack in front of all those young kids and the teenagers, including his own children. My wife, traumatized by the scene, never wanted to go back. And even though we did travel with P and her family from time to time, spending a weekend together in the countryside, we'd never gone to visit them on that island.

"And I don't really like swimming in pools," P added, as if she'd been listening to my thoughts.

"Why not?"

"There's no life, in that water."

We talked about other seas, other islands, the pleasures of boating versus going to the beach: the frivolous patter of people with money. But as we spoke we became aware that a strange calm had descended over the yard. The children weren't yelling anymore. Something had happened.

· 4 ·

We went down to see. A group of kids, a dozen or so, stood frozen in the distance. In the middle of their circle, someone was lying on the ground.

As we inched closer, we saw a handsome young boy, twelve or so, his hair disheveled, legs splayed—it didn't look good. Had he fainted? Or had something worse happened? We had no information. Then the doctor arrived, the one who'd saved P's life years before. A tall, lanky man with black hair grazing his shoulders, a dangling mustache, a steady, good-natured demeanor.

Next to the boy was a pale-faced woman. The mother, I assumed. I hadn't noticed her before—we hadn't crossed paths, despite having just spent at least an hour in the same crowded house, in the same rooms, circling the same table, eating the same food.

She was a foreigner, you could tell right away by her facial features. She was wearing a summery dress unsuited to the season; a heavy and complicated necklace adorned a triangle of bare skin. She wore very little makeup—with the exception of wine-colored nail polish—and had a kind of prematurely weathered beauty. Her dark hair was tied up in a bun at her nape. She must have been around ten years younger than my wife, with a sharper gaze and, I felt, a more turbulent inner life.

"What happened?" the doctor asked her.

"I have no idea. I was inside while he was playing. Then one of his friends came and told me he wasn't feeling well. By the time I got here he was trembling—he seemed shaken and disoriented."

The woman spoke in a strange mix of her language and ours, but it was easy enough to follow.

"And then?"

"He said his head was spinning, and that he couldn't hear anything for a few seconds, that everything went silent."

"Give us a little space, please," the doctor said.

The crowd backed off. Only the boy and his mother remained, with the doctor and P. I took a few steps back myself, but then I froze, paralyzed by the thought that the same thing could just as easily happen to my son—why not?—playing soccer in the park on a Sunday, with no parent at his side.

No one spoke for a minute or two. The doctor examined the boy, lifted his feet, felt his forehead, his wrist. After a little while, the boy sat up on his own and had a sip of water.

"It's not too serious, *signora*," the doctor explained.

"But why? He's always been an active boy, nothing like this has ever happened."

"Your son suffered a mild shock. Perhaps he didn't eat enough lunch. Kids are always running around nonstop without thinking. This kind of thing can happen sometimes when we get overexcited. Did your son have breakfast this morning?"

"Yes."

"Is he an anxious boy?"

I got the impression that she didn't understand the question. In any case, she didn't respond. Her son was back on his feet now, a little embarrassed, insisting he was fine. His speech was normal. He had braces. He'd accepted a sandwich from someone and was eating.

"Can I keep playing?" he asked the doctor. Unlike his mother, he spoke our language perfectly well, and even had a touch of our city's accent.

"Of course you can. Just take it easy."

And that was that. The party went on. We went back inside, they brought out the cake, we sang "Happy Birthday," raised our glasses to P. Her kids gave her a stiff gold bracelet. Then there was a real surprise: her husband stood on a chair and sang a short, sweet love song out of tune, while P, overwhelmed, in tears, burst out laughing, then gave her husband a long kiss, eyes closed, in front of everyone.

The crowd inside the house began to thin, guests were starting to leave. I rejoined my wife, who told me that she, too, was ready to head home. We said our goodbyes to P and her husband, thanked them for the pleasant afternoon, and returned to our car, where we waited for the long line ahead of us to budge.

"It's late. Did you have fun?" my wife asked me.

"I had a pretty good time. How about you?"

"Did you drink?"

"Not much."

She looked me up and down.

"Let me drive."

I was tired, and handed her the keys without protest. We switched places. She adjusted the seat, the mirror. She put on her seat belt, the comfortable shoes she liked to drive in. She was just about to start the car when she realized that she'd left her shawl in the house.

"I don't feel like getting out. Will you go?"

"Any idea where it is?"

"Check on the patio—I think I draped it over the back of a chair."

The house was empty, silent, filled with abandoned glasses and soiled, crumpled paper napkins. P and her family must have retired to one room or another. My wife was right, the shawl was there, hanging limp as a fresh sheet of pasta over the back of a patio chair, not far from where I'd listened to P rave about her island, before the boy felt sick.

The boy's mother was standing in front of me—facing away, but I recognized her immediately, her hair in a bun, her taut neck. She was alone, staring at the yard, where a handful of kids, including her son, were still out playing. She was smoking a cigarette. When she turned to see who was there, she, too, seemed to recognize me right away. From the blanched look on her face I could tell she was still distraught.

"What exactly does 'a mild shock' even mean?" she asked me at once.

"A state of confusion perhaps. A moment of psychosomatic distress."

"I thought he was going to die. In the middle of a party, at this house filled with people I barely know."

"Don't worry, it's over now, I heard what the doctor said." I addressed her with the formal pronoun.

"I used to be such a centered person. I knew how to run my life. But these days, in this country, I can hardly manage a thing."

"How did you end up here?"

"My husband is a journalist. He likes Rome. He says he loves this city more than he loves me."

"And you, how do you like it?"

"I'm not happy and I'm not unhappy. Mind if we use the *tu*?"

"Of course."

"Why did you stay with my son and me the whole time?"

"What do you mean?"

"On the grass. You didn't walk away with the others."

"I was worried, like you. That's all."

"Do you also have a son?"

"Yes. He lives abroad."

"So you'll understand."

"Understand what?"

"Today I brushed up against the worst thing that could possibly happen."

· 5 ·

For the next few days I was left reeling from that abrupt exchange of words. Who was that woman? Why had she been so open with me, so unguarded, instantly bridging the solitary distance between two strangers? Why had she revealed to me, out of the blue, that she was in crisis? What was her name? When and how had she met P? Where was this husband she'd spoken of, who loved Rome more than he loved her?

One evening, after some hesitation, I asked my wife: "Did you meet anyone interesting at P's this year?"

"Not really. Sometimes I have no patience for meeting new people."

"There were so many foreigners, more every year."

"They must be the parents of her kids' friends, who go to the same international school."

"A good school?"

"Expensive, and a little overrated if you ask me. I trust our school system."

Then she told me about a friend of ours—he, too, a regular at P's yearly party—who was thinking of quitting his job as the dean of a small suburban university to open a wine store in a foreign capital.

It would have been inappropriate to turn to P for any information. My wife was probably right, the woman who'd spoken to me was most likely the mother of one of P's kids' classmates. The more I thought about our conversation on the patio, the more I was struck by our strange synchronicity in that moment, as if she were expecting me, as if she knew, beforehand, that my wife would have forgotten her shawl, and that she'd send me back to the house to retrieve it. In the end, it was the only conversation of any real substance I'd had at the party. We'd looked each other in the eye, we'd been alone, our bodies close, but I'd never even introduced myself. I'd grabbed my wife's shawl, mumbled something awkward, and then I'd slipped away.

Over time, the memory began to dim. I went on living with my wife, in the house where we'd raised our son. I made love to her still slender body, I invited the same friends over for dinner, cooked the same reliable recipes. While my wife went to the gallery or away on the occasional business trip, I worked at home, in the corner of our bedroom, making slow progress on my fifth novel, my articles, my tepid reviews. When she returned in the evenings, I'd pour us some wine and pretend to listen while she gave me the full rundown of her complicated days. On Saturdays, once a month, we'd go to hear classical music, then out to a restaurant, or else to the opening of a new art exhibit. I would go to the library, and we'd go on vacation: to the mountains every year, for her birthday, and to the sea, in the off-season, for mine.

At Christmas we traveled abroad to visit our son. He showed us his drab studio apartment, where he lived happily, and introduced us to his first girlfriend, an attractive young woman with parents from two different continents. He'd met her at the university. The two of them took us to a sprawling, noisy restaurant they loved. I noticed that my son, taller than I was now, was looking bulkier even though he'd become a vegetarian. He preferred beer over wine. The photo of a gawky boy that greeted me every time I picked up my cell phone, taken on a fishing boat the previous summer, looked nothing like him anymore.

Because of the girlfriend, we never spoke to each other in Italian. He gushed about the multiethnic neighborhood where they lived, where they'd go out every night of the week to eat food from seven different countries. His answers to my questions were polite but brief. We conversed in a language I struggled to keep up with, a sensation that I enjoyed at P's house but that here, with my own son, felt frustrating and artificial. For Easter, he told me, he planned to go hiking with his girlfriend among castles and sheep. In the course of a day or two I could sense his tacit rejection not only of Rome but of our way of life, of all the effort we'd put into raising him a certain way.

He was thriving in this new city—but, even so, I didn't like the thought of him in that drab apartment, at those loud restaurants, eating bizarre and expensive food, with his wisp of a girlfriend smiling beside him. I didn't like the thought of him in the crush of a subway car, or walking the streets alone and a little drunk at three in the morning, or going to the park on Sundays to play soccer with no breakfast in his stomach. I worried that he wasn't mature enough, that deep down he felt unhappy, that he'd end up in some kind of trouble. But that naïve and vulnerable boy was not my son: he was me. Or rather, he was the version of me I'd never allowed to form, that I'd neglected, blocked out—a version that, even without ever having existed, had defeated me. With this thought in my head, I strolled around my son's new city, patiently admiring bridges, gardens, and monuments, beneath a low and leaden sky.

On the plane, before taking off, watching my wife check her email on her phone, I realized that it was just the two of us again, except this time with no desire to have a child, without that life project to tie us together, as it had until now. What was she reading? Who was writing to her? Hundreds of messages poured in every day from mysterious senders. A densely inhabited world, buzzing with activity, hers alone. But at a certain point she raised her head and reminded me of the date for P's next party.

· 6 ·

Only once we were in the car, on the way to P's house, did I recall that distraught mother, that unexpected confession on the patio. It had been nearly a year since I'd thought of her. I'd left my curiosity back at P's, as if it were an umbrella, or the shawl my wife had asked me to retrieve: the kind of thing

whose absence you feel for a little while and then easily let go
of. But now that I was about to return to that house, again I
sensed that she and I shared some secret link.

My foot was heavy on the gas, I was distracted. I missed
the sharp right turn, took another road, had to put the car in
reverse, as my wife's irritation grew. I was thinking: I should
have chosen a different shirt, the one I'm wearing doesn't do
much for me. The agitation I'd experienced after the abrupt
exchange on the patio was back. I could picture it clearly now,
the flattering but unseasonable dress, the complicated necklace, the color of her fingernail polish. As if the year gone by
were nothing, nothing the passage of time. We hadn't even
shaken hands, there was just that flash of understanding. So
why was I feeling a little guilty?

An ancient, ridiculous memory came back to me then, from
just before I met my wife. I was going to a gym with a pool
at the time, and every week, by the pool's edge, the same girl
would smile at me and say hello. She swam in the lane that I'd
take over. For a few months my entire week revolved around
that brief encounter by the pool, to the point where I'd even
rush to the locker room to make sure I didn't miss her. We
never talked about anything. She'd just say *Have a good swim,*
or something like that. But every time she looked at me and
spoke to me, it felt as if I were the center of her world. We ran
into each other in this way for a few months, then she stopped
showing up. A couple of months later I met my wife—but
early on, in bed, I'd picture the swimmer's eyes, her smile.
That's all.

Parking the car, I thought: Maybe the distraught woman
won't even be here, maybe she wasn't invited this time around,

or maybe she had another engagement. Her presence was hardly a given. But as soon as we entered, after P and her husband had welcomed us in, as my wife was already chatting without me in the adjoining room, I caught sight of her.

She was sitting in the dining room, beneath a window, in one of the chairs lined up against the wall so that guests could circulate. Next to her was her husband—a tall, handsome man with shiny white hair, a young-looking face, tan even in January. It had to be her husband because they were sharing a plate of food; that way, each could hold a glass of wine in the other hand. She wasn't talking to him. She was turned toward two other women seated to her right—but there was too much noise, I could barely even make out her voice.

She was utterly changed. She was laughing, telling a funny anecdote about herself, while her husband listened and held the plate. He seemed like an attentive guy, amiable but a little bit tense. She was speaking with abandon, with irony. She didn't strike me at all as a woman in crisis.

She was dressed in black, like nearly all the other women at the party. No necklace, just that triangle of bare skin. She wore a pair of tight-fitting pants that matched the season, and hammered leather boots. Her hair, longer now, was streaked with gray, which she clearly didn't mind. She was thinner, even more beautiful—that weathered sort of beauty, which flattered her. Like my son, she had morphed over the past year into a sunnier, more confident version of herself. We lived in the same not particularly large city, and yet we'd never bumped into each other, not in a restaurant, not at a pharmacy, not on the street or at the gym. Our paths crossed only at this house, only at P's party.

"Hey, we're on the patio, it's nice out there," an old friend said, running into me.

"Be there in a minute."

I made a leisurely loop around the table, picking up some cheese, some crudités, some sliced salami. I was trying to make my presence felt. I couldn't hear her, all I could hear was my wife's gravelly voice, which worked its way under my skin even amid all those people.

When her husband stood to find a trash can where he could toss their plate, I looked at her, waiting for her to look back. Hoping for what, I don't know—a smile like the one the girl would give me by the side of the pool? But she remained absorbed in her anecdote.

I continued staring, and she kept talking. Her husband was gone, my wife in the next room. The more I looked, the more she evaded me, unfazed. Until all of a sudden she lifted her gaze, for an instant, and revealed her eyes to me—filled (I thought) with fury and exasperation, blinding eyes that were shining (I hoped) for me.

· 7 ·

The idea appealed to me: a relationship punctuated with gaps; a fixed date, ours alone, in the middle of the party. It seemed like an acceptable form of infidelity, entirely forgivable, a bit like when I thought of the girl from the pool while I was already with my wife. In truth I wasn't looking for trouble. Just a few blazing hours spent together, checked by a year of separation.

I'd never betrayed my wife in this city, where everyone's

always cheating on everyone. With the exception of my little crush on the girl from the pool, I'd always been a faithful man; I was used to being the one who got dumped or cheated on, even before I met my wife, and not the other way around. I didn't have infidelity in me, I suppose I lacked the impulse. I accepted my wife's activities, her obligations—the constant messages on her phone, her dinners without me, her work trips abroad, her quick jaunts to other cities—while also admitting the likely consequences: a quickly forgotten one-night stand with some guy, lunch and a stroll through the botanical garden with another. But since I wasn't jealous by nature, my conjectures never took hold of me. As with any couple, things left unsaid enter in to maintain your aging affection. Which was how we'd survived twenty-three years together with no major disruptions, no earthquakes.

I repeat, I'd have been fine dragging out that trifling dalliance. But just a few months later my wife informed me that P was having another party.

"So soon? What's that about?"

"She said she's been teaching her oldest son to dance, which got her thinking that she'd like to throw a different kind of party. At night this time. No kids."

"Did we ever teach our son to dance?"

"Maybe?"

"Do you know who's coming?"

"The usual slew of people, I imagine."

· 8 ·

The weather was terrible that evening. I felt queasy the entire day. I couldn't eat, couldn't concentrate at my desk.

"It's been a long week, I can't shake this headache," I said to my wife.

"And so . . . ?"

"What do you say we stay in for the night?"

I already knew my suggestion was futile. She was taking her time getting ready, wearing a short dress she hadn't pulled out in years.

"Tonight we dance and let go. Time to perk up."

In the dark, P's house seemed like a new destination—even more out of the way, more alien. The drive was stressful, the charming road slick with rain. And the spring air felt wrong to me. I couldn't get my bearings.

"Did you hear that their house was robbed recently?" my wife said as I was parking the car behind a long line of vehicles.

"Who?"

"P's family. They were gone for three days, all the jewelry was taken."

"They didn't have it in a safe?"

"No, unfortunately, she's always been a bit disorganized."

The house, too, was nearly dark, unfamiliar. They'd removed most of the furniture to make room. P's daughter greeted us at the door and whisked our coats off to who knows where. I stuck to my wife's side. We went to get our first glass of prosecco together, to fill our plastic plates with slices of bread, slivers of cheese, honey. We were attached at the hip as if we were a shy couple on an early date.

I saw all the known and unknown faces that were always at P's. Apart from the new setup, the empty rooms, the scene was more or less identical, and yet I couldn't manage to wedge my way into conversations as I usually did; searching for that woman left me discombobulated. She was standing next to her husband, on the other side of the room. And this time she didn't avoid my gaze. She was looking straight at me through the crowd, registering my presence without smiling, without budging, without communicating anything.

After dinner the dancing began. P's older son chose the music, a string of inane songs from our younger days. I danced with my wife, the woman with her husband. P's other kids danced between us, they danced with P and her husband. P danced with my wife, and then with me. She was a little drunk, barefoot, affectionate, shimmering, even without a bit of jewelry on. I really love you two, she said to me and my wife, as the three of us danced together.

The music felt liberating, at moments wrenching. It levitated us magically above the cramped and craggy present, it restored a glimmer of hope. We were, all of us, each on our own, replaying our previous lives: lives still in progress, foolish, makeshift, splendid lives. I glanced around at the women who refused to play the role of *signora,* who'd kept up their looks. And yet we weren't getting any younger, we were accumulating wrinkles, health scares, disappointments. The songs took us back—to our first kiss, our first relationship, ancient emotions, our first heartbreak, minor grievances we'd buried, unresolved, but had never shaken off.

She and I danced, together, on our own. It was a torment, also a triumph. We would lock eyes for a moment, here and there I'd feel my body brushing hers, a shoulder, a hip. The two of us were still nailed to our respective lives, but underneath it all I sensed that we were being reckless, conspiratorial.

Outside it was still raining, but inside it was hot, oppressively hot. I was covered in sweat. I told my wife I could use a little water. I went to the bathroom, rinsed my face. Then I went to the kitchen to find a glass. There I noticed a complex surveillance system mounted on the wall, for monitoring the house's entry points. It had multiple tiny screens, each with a different view: the front gate, the yard, the patio. At night, in the heavy rain, every image looked to me like a kind of ominous ultrasound, ripe with meaning but completely indecipherable.

When I returned, I noticed that the lights were on. The barren room, only recently vacated, reminded me in some ways of my son's apartment. No one was dancing anymore, the music had stopped. In the old days we'd have merely taken a break, but we were already worn out.

My wife was over by the table. She was eating dessert. And she was talking to her. They didn't notice me. My wife said, "I was just admiring your necklace while we were dancing, it's extraordinary. Can I ask where you bought it?"

"In a cute little shop, not far from where we live."

"How long have you two lived in Rome?"

"Three years now."

"Are you here for work?"

"My husband, yes. He'd like to live here forever."

"What about you?"

She shrugged. "Forever is a big word."

They went to grab their purses, they pulled out their phones. Right there on the spot they exchanged numbers, scheduled a date.

· 9 ·

And this is where my story takes an unexpected turn. This stranger, with whom I'd had only one conversation, a fevered and fragmentary exchange, and with whom I'd felt an inexplicable bond from that moment on, despite never having learned her name, became my wife's friend. They met for lunch once a month, then went shopping for clothes and shoes together. She remained a secondary, casual friend for my wife. Not someone she'd invite over to the apartment, or fold into our everyday lives, but a person she'd spend time with on her own now and then, in her own way.

Through their friendship I learned a few things: her name—L—and the neighborhood where she lived (San Giovanni). One day she mentioned how often her husband had to travel, racing back and forth between cities. They had one son, the boy who'd fallen sick in the yard. As my wife had intuited, he went to the same school as one of P's sons. L used to have a job herself, as a magazine editor, but here she spent her days diligently studying our language and belonged to a group of foreign women who relentlessly visited the city's infinite monuments, attractions, and ruins. Apart from these details my wife never spoke of her new friendship.

I knew that it was normal, even healthy, to cultivate these kinds of friendships outside a marriage. It wasn't like there was anything sexual involved. And yet I agonized over it. My writing suffered, I began missing deadlines for my projects, I envied my wife.

I envied my wife and yet at the same time I was grateful. There was no way, when they went out together on their walks or to see an art exhibit, that L didn't think of me. No way my wife didn't speak of me, of our long marriage filled with the predictable ups and downs, of the flings she'd probably had with other men, of our strained relationship with our son. No way I didn't factor in to some extent. After more than twenty years of marriage, I knew what happened when women talked—all that archived information which loosens in the vapor of friendship, which floats to the surface while they're out buying shoes, eating salads, admiring paintings.

But what was I hoping for? An actual affair with L? A date, a few hours in a hotel, in bed together? I don't think so. Even after the dancing I never thought of her body, her hands. What I fixated on was our conversation on the patio, when she was distraught, sick with worry over her son, when she confided in me. That moment seemed more transgressive than any erotic act. What had we shared? An intimate exchange, inexplicably charged. And now, just as inexplicably, we shared my wife.

Soon enough the spring had gone by, an entire season. I remained passive, cagey, lying in wait for a new development: a dinner together, plans for a night at the theater with L and her husband. But what I was really waiting for was winter, and P's next party, even if—and it was clear by now—those spirited occasions, those restorative afternoons I held so dear, were tainted.

· 10 ·

But late that summer, once again, P suddenly changed the script. My wife and I were already back from vacation, had stashed away our bathing suits and beach towels and sandals. For my own part, I was looking forward to the firm and reassuring light of autumn, the plates of puntarelle at the trattorie, the starlings that dart in the sky, appearing and disappearing like tornadoes or ribbons or giant tadpoles made of ash, when P offered us a last-minute invitation to the island where she and her family spent two months each year. She had access to a spare bungalow with an ocean view—the usual tenants had canceled—and she was certain that it would make an ideal spot for my writing, having heard from my wife that I'd been in a long slump.

"You know, I wouldn't mind going back there either, finally putting an end to my childhood fear," my wife announced, referring to that poor man she'd seen die in the pool, decades earlier.

And given that it was a particularly stifling summer, and that my wife and I really had nothing to do but idle around the apartment, we packed our suitcases again, drove down to the harbor, and boarded a ferry. The island was a rock in the middle of nowhere, a bit like P's house.

For several days we did nothing but enjoy luxuriant, late-morning swims, light and refreshing lunches, and sunset strolls down to the lighthouse. The water was as clear as glass, filled with dark sea urchins. A beautiful path ran the length of the island, but in certain stretches you had to beware of clefts in the rock. Once, P told us, a woman had fallen to her death while taking a photo of her husband. We floated around the island on a rubber dinghy and ate baked fish on the terrace, with coils and citronella candles to repel the mosquitoes.

P and my wife took the boat every day, either before or after lunch, to pick up groceries. They wore flared linen dresses, and always came back with a little something extra: a clever bracelet made of cork, a perfume that smelled of salt, silicone kitchen utensils in various colors. They cooked together, reminiscing about the happy years when they'd shared an apartment, before they were married and had kids. P's husband came out on the weekend but left again for work. The kids played Ping-Pong all day or horsed around on the beach, tried out reckless dives at the pool, or wandered off alone to some secret spot.

Our bungalow was very charming, picturesque, a bit dim inside but airy. It had belonged to one of P's uncles, he, too, a writer, and I discovered many old, well-loved books there, marked up in pencil. It was a cozy space, masculine in feeling, just one room, really, with no kitchen and one square window that looked out on the sea and opened like the door to a cupboard. The furniture had never been replaced—soft, faded armchairs, dark, glossy wood, a musty smell, all of it frozen in time.

As soon as I stepped inside I felt better; the space was invigorating, and had an effect on me similar to that of P's house, except here there was no party. This was a refuge where I could hole up and concentrate. Which got me thinking, a bit peeved: It would have been truly ideal to have had a place like this at our disposal, a place to write, if only my wife hadn't been avoiding this island, if only she'd brought me here before. Our son would have liked it, too, in the past, but now there was no room here for him and his girlfriend, there were just two couches, one across from the other, that became beds—two separate singles, one for me and one for my wife.

As soon as we were settled in, I hit a stride with my writing, hunched over a tiny desk against a wall, or else lying back on one of the sofa beds. I skipped lunch with P and my wife, instead grabbing a sandwich at the snack bar around three, my mind humming. I was pleased with this second summer of ours, with the inspiration I found on that island, in that cozy and comfortable bungalow.

The mistral arrived, as expected: three days of nonstop wind, of deafening gusts. On the storm's first day I started a new short story about L, set at P's house. In my invented version things took a more predictable course: she and I had a real affair. Staring out at the white shelf of sea lashing the shore, I thought back to our conversation on the patio—in the fake version we kissed immediately—looking for ways to stretch the details. I inserted the scene where we danced together, and also on our own—it felt like a critical juncture in the plot—and I left out L's friendship with my wife, which proved an unwieldy development. I molded and massaged the facts until it felt like a vaguely appealing story, the kind a literary magazine might take. All I needed was the ending, the grand finale.

One morning I decided to go for a swim, to clear out my head before sitting down to write. The mistral had just moved on and the water was once again a sheet of glass. I climbed in from a small sheltered cove, first checking for jellyfish. My destination was a red buoy, which I swam toward through a beautiful patch of green sea, following a school of minnows. I was out in the middle of that patch when I saw a motorboat heading straight at me. I stopped and waved an arm, but the boat kept coming. I didn't shout, it would have been pointless. Out that far, all sounds are swallowed by the sea's silence. Feeling slow, weak, frightened, I somehow managed to move out of the way, and I made it to shore.

I walked back to the house, stricken pale, still unnerved. But my wife wasn't there, and P's place was empty, too. On the little desk was a note: *Out getting groceries, catch up with you later.* My head was spinning. I felt like I needed a fresh glass of orange juice. At the snack bar I ran into one of P's boys, the thirteen-year-old.

"How's it going, all good?" he asked.

"A boat nearly ran me over."

"Were you swimming alone?"

"I was."

"Best to stay close to shore."

"What about you guys? You having fun?"

"It gets a bit boring. I'd like to go somewhere else next year, but my mom always wants to come here."

"Hang in there."

"At least my friend's coming tonight."

"Oh, who's that?"

"This foreign kid I go to school with. He's on a boat trip with his parents, his dad's a really good navigator. They're stopping at the island and staying for dinner."

· 1 1 ·

At sunset we walked down to the harbor to greet them. It was a beautiful motorboat. They were dropping the fenders. Her husband was at the helm, her son hanging their wet things on a drying rack, L clambering around the boat. She was moving swiftly, asking her husband what to do before they docked. She was wearing a special pair of gloves for handling the anchor chain. I admired how deftly she tied and untied the mooring line. I noticed the ease and economy of communication between husband and wife.

With the task complete and the motor spent, they said their hellos. L had picked up a tan, her husband, too. Their son had outgrown both his parents. I glimpsed L's dark, muscular legs, a scar on her thigh. She was barefoot, sweaty, her hair a windblown mess. She quickly slipped into a sheer beach cover-up, a pair of elegant but well-worn sandals.

I wanted to break up the scene right then and there. I wanted to sneak down into the cabin, on that boat, with her. As if driven by the mistral, like the waves beating steadily in one direction, an impulse intensified by my own imagined version of our affair, I now yearned to kiss her mouth, to taste her salty skin, to solidify our connection at last without having to share it with anyone else. Instead, when she stepped off the boat, we greeted each other with a handshake, and all she said to me was "Ciao."

We took our seats out on P's terrace. There were five of us—P's husband would be back the next day, and L's son had rushed off to meet his friend in the small piazza. We spoke in Italian. By now, after all their meticulous studying, L and her husband could speak it more or less fluently. The windstorm had swept away the mosquitoes. The air felt crisp, refreshing. I was sitting next to L, at the head of the table, with P and my wife on one side and L and her husband across from them.

We drank heavily that night, though L a bit less than we did, since she was suffering from land sickness. Her husband weighed in on the recent elections, and told of their boating adventures, describing their favorite islands and inlets. At sea, he said, you live with less but have it all.

We ate a rice salad, followed by some fish and a few slices of melon. L passed me the fruit, the bottle of mirto. And while we ate and talked, while we looked at the stars and listened to the waves, while my eyes strayed now and then to that same triangle of bare skin, that extraordinary divot of flesh outlined by her collarbone and shoulders, I learned something new. In a month they'd be returning to their country; their time in Italy had come to an end. The reasons they gave were practical: her husband was tired of the constant travel, their son was about to start his first year of high school, and L, it turned out, was missing the working life that she'd sacrificed to be here. They were sad to go, already speaking with nostalgia about certain things, but you could see that the decision to reactivate their old life had restored the family balance, and that the cliff's edge they were once teetering on was no longer a threat.

"Maybe we'll come back around New Year's. It would be nice to get a little winter sun, have some panettone and pandoro, eat lunch outdoors in January."

"Perfect. That means you'll be here for my party," P said.

We accompanied them back to the harbor, said our goodbyes on the dock. "Ciao," L said to me again—nothing else—and in that moment of confusion I kissed her, at first on the cheek, but then my mouth drifted down toward the salty skin of her collarbone, planting itself in that sunken triangle. I latched on to her for a few seconds, then I lifted my head, mortified, and muttered, "Forgive me."

She immediately stepped back. And she may have glared at me then as she had once before, her eyes filled with fury and exasperation, but it was too dark to tell.

After she hugged and thanked everyone else, after she said her goodbyes to my wife and P, she left with her family to spend the night on their boat, by a secluded grotto, in a tiny cabin beside her husband. My wife, meanwhile, who'd glimpsed that errant kiss, started haranguing me as soon as we entered the bungalow and kept at it until dawn.

"Is there something going on with you two?"

"Nothing, I barely know her."

"You imbecile, she was my friend."

"And she still is."

"I doubt it. The whole reason I came out here was to lay down an old burden, and now, thanks to you, I've picked up another."

"I'm sorry."

My wife refused to calm down. She went on attacking me, then burst into tears, transforming my creative sanctuary into a hell.

· 12 ·

The next day, earlier than planned, we, too, left the island, in a rush. There was no need to explain our departure to P, given that I'd kissed L in front of her and her children, too. The whole lot of them were witnesses—and, worse, even with the whistling wind and the crashing waves, they'd probably heard us fighting until dawn. For days, back in the city, I cursed my own stupidity, steeped in embarrassment, but my wife never brought it up again, and soon the unpleasant feeling faded.

We fell back into our old routines, though for months I was adrift. I abandoned the short story—with those pages, I realized, I'd been luring myself onto a precipice. What had happened between L and me made for a dull premise, it never would have worked. Yet for a moment, on that island, my embellished version of events had fused with reality: it had driven me to wound and demean my wife, in a way that she, with her discreet behavior, had never done to me in our long years of marriage.

I'd already decided, before Christmas, that I wouldn't be going to P's party that winter. On the off chance that L and her family were in town, I had my excuse prepared. But then, just before Christmas, P got sick again. Her decline was rapid, until the same good doctor who'd saved her life said there was nothing left to do.

Soon thereafter, I found myself at the funeral, and afterward at the house where we'd celebrated P so many times. Yet again on a bright and balmy winter day. A Saturday afternoon, a few weeks before her birthday, with all the guests from her previous parties, all of her closest friends.

My wife was devastated, she'd practically lost a sister. We clasped hands before entering the house. All the women, wearing black, were stone-faced. P's children, who'd been so drunk with joy on the island, who'd had so much fun that summer, were standing still in a row, in one of the rooms. The littlest one started weeping when my wife went to hug her.

"It was important to her, the party," her husband said to me. "She looked forward to it every year."

"Me, too," I replied.

We spoke about P. About how she was a singular person, a singular woman, radiant, the only one with the strength to bring us all together. To open the door a thousand times, to fill the house and churn the crowd.

Aside from the absence of P and her hospitality, things were essentially the same. The funeral, too, was a kind of party. The kids, after a while, went out to play in the yard. Food covered the big oval table in the room with many windows, all the chairs lined up against the walls so that guests could circulate.

We ate, we conversed. But in the wake of a death even your own breath, your own shadow come as a shock. Everything feels inappropriate, indecent, for a while.

This would be the last time we ever set foot in that house. It was already up for sale. P's husband, her children, couldn't bear to live in it anymore.

L wasn't there. Which didn't surprise me. As a peripheral figure, an occasional guest, she wasn't invited to the funeral. I saw only a few members of her group, the people who spoke other languages, who passed in and out of our lives. Just like P, whatever had happened between us—that stalemate, that nonstarter, brought to an end by my foolish gesture—was no longer.

I can't complain. Unlike me, P, to whom I owe these pages, didn't make it out of the story. She'll never visit her children in other countries, or cry about distances or the passing of days, that merciless, automatic plot device that propels us forward and brings us to our knees. Her parties, however, have stayed with me, and the thought of them still quickens the heart: the secluded house packed with people, the sunlit lawn, those hours of sublime detachment. A setting I cherished, a promising start I tried to finish, to put into words, in which I'd been, briefly, a wayward husband, an inspired author, a happy man.

Well-Lit House

A WELL-LIT HOUSE can change your life.

After we moved there in the spring with our five children—ages two, four, six, seven, and nine—my wife worried less about escalators that nip at your legs, tremors at dawn that shake open closet doors, wobbly market umbrellas that tip over just five feet away while you're calmly selecting tomatoes from a stall in the piazza, and sick, untended trees with severed or rotting roots that come crashing down in the middle of the street and land on cars and people.

One day, while out pushing one of our children in the stroller, she witnessed a pine tree collapse and kill a hapless stranger: a man sitting bored in his car, probably waiting for someone, checking messages on his cell phone. My wife stood there in shock for more than an hour, as if she'd lost a loved one, until the carabinieri and firemen came to extract his body and take it away. The car, she later told me, looked like a plastic bottle crushed between your hands before recycling it, to save space in the bin. She holed up in the house for weeks, unnerved and unwilling to go out anywhere with the kids.

· · ·

IN THAT HOUSE, though, east of the city, she no longer fret-
ted over dangers lying everywhere in wait, horrors printed in
the newspaper that could eventually happen to anyone. Not
even the piercing whine of the kettle when the hot water was
ready bothered her anymore, nor the whining and whimper-
ing of our children—three boys, the oldest sweet-tempered
and stick-thin, the second a little chubby, the third already
wearing glasses, and between them our two bright-eyed little
girls, both with their mother's delicate, perfectly curved eyebrows and lips—who were always turning the rooms upside
down.

Our apartment, on the first floor, was only five hundred
square feet, but for the first time we had our own tiny bedroom, where the morning sun poured in, where we'd wake to
that rush of light and the birds exchanging their secret messages, incomprehensible in our world. We liked the soft sheets
and, whenever the children were napping and we managed to
push the door shut, a white light would bathe our souls while
we made love. We even joked of having a sixth child. The air in
that house was in constant motion, which saved us during that
prematurely hot spring. It felt almost like the beach, inside.
We could even hear the occasional seagull. A real beach, we
said to each other in amazement, as if we were on vacation, by
the sea, without the hassle of sand or jellyfish, but always with
that same light that warms your bones and, if you close your
eyes, lets you see that phosphorescent red behind your eyelids.

· · ·

THERE WAS SKY to spare on the city's outskirts, a truly infinite sky; at times, despite all the construction and the heaps of cement, it felt more like we were in the country than in the city. Some trees, not many. But along the roadsides the rush grew in massive clumps, with tall, sharp blades all leaning the same way, like spears ready to be hurled by a vast army in a world still ruled by hand-to-hand combat. A bit of drug dealing down in the street, but never mind, you see that kind of thing downtown, even in fancier piazzas where tourists flock.

Thrilled about the move, we paid no mind to our neighbor's warning. An elderly widow with a slight hunch, she'd approached us while we were busy carrying boxes up and down, a tray of coffee and a Bundt cake in her unsteady hands shot through with dark green veins. She'd admired the way my wife's veil framed her face, saying it made her look like the noblewomen from long ago, the ones you see in faded or darkened paintings in churches and museums. And she'd put us on alert about the neighborhood—it could be a little sketchy, she said, and we seemed to her like a nice family.

BUT EVEN WHEN you have everything you've dreamed of, you still want more, and once we'd settled into the apartment, with our clothes in the cupboards, forks in the drawer, and a plant on the windowsill in the kitchen, we thought of how nice it would be if we too had a little balcony like the ones on the building next to ours—something modest, just large enough to hold a few more plants. On the balcony we could see from our bedroom, my wife noticed a fuchsia hibiscus stem jutting out on its own, like some glorious fishing rod dangling over the sky. She'd like to be that flowering stem, she told me, swaying in peace: vibrant, free, cradled and sustained by nothing but air. In the mornings, pigeons would come with twigs in their mouths, to build their nest beside the crank for extending or retracting the awning. Under the awning was a white metal table, but we never saw anyone eating or chatting there at sunset. Just a lady in slippers, once, who took up a broom and, with a certain satisfaction, swept away the nest.

In that house, for the first time, I too felt protected from the city and from our neighborhood filled with residents and shopkeepers who tolerated our presence only to a certain extent. The butcher, for example, who cut our meat without ever asking my wife, with her dress that hung to her feet and her head draped by a veil—the only way she felt comfortable going out—how she was planning to prepare the chicken or liver, as he did with the other ladies. Otherwise it struck us as a place without incident, walled off by the thick, tall rush. There was a large hospital at one end, a train station at the other. The hospital took up a giant lot, its entrance facing a street with heavy traffic, while the mortuary, on a parallel street, was a little more secluded. Between them were various pavilions, walkways, bushes, and flower beds, forming a kind of miniature city. Tall gates stood at the entrance, but anyone could walk through, so we went for a stroll there a couple of times with the kids, as if one of our relatives were a patient inside. We even sat on a bench to admire the brilliant oleanders, the scented magnolias, and I smoked a cigarette while the children played hide-and-seek. Sure, there were some off-putting things graffitied on a few of the buildings nearby, and on the walls surrounding the hospital, but nothing you wouldn't find anywhere else.

In that house, stretched out on the bed, I'd stare at the edge of the weathered awning, the one on the balcony of the building next to ours, with the bird nest and the hibiscus stem that my wife liked so much. The border of the awning would ripple almost constantly in the wind. The fabric was all faded, and several strands hung down like hairs or tufts of grass. The scalloped border originally created a series of equal-sized waves, each one identical. Now all the waves were different, some of them split in two, forming gaps that made them seem like a kind of theater curtain, or a sacred sheet of papyrus chewed up by time, like the ones the man sold at the flea market where I worked on Sundays. Here and there the hem of the border had detached, creating a kind of hollow eye filled with sky; and occasionally, when the wind picked up and ruffled the fabric, it would lift that absence, too.

When I stared at that awning, tattered and fluttering, I'd stop thinking about the war or the soldiers who'd killed my grandparents, or the journey to this country afterward with my parents, white butterflies flitting above the sea's surface, a frantic but cheerful swarm traveling alongside us, almost seeming to lead the way.

At first we lived in a camp, then in a trailer or wherever else we could. Which meant I grew up in different places across the city, each one forgettable, along with my parents, my brothers, and the relatives who arrived periodically, one after another. On Saturdays I helped my father at the flea market, fixing watches, replacing batteries or the strap or the entire mechanism. Hordes of people came to throw their money away on mostly useless objects.

I was still young when my father died. Unfortunately I hadn't learned how to repair watches, so I started selling clothes: socks, underwear, nightgowns. During the weekdays I made deliveries for a few places, furniture, heavy boxes, appliances, but on Sundays I also started giving a hand to the used book salesman. He'd thrown his back out picking tobacco in the past, so he'd have me load the car, set up the tent, and break down the booth at the end of the day. There were people who'd pay absurd amounts for certain books, even if an insect had been crushed between the pages, the stain still gleaming.

When I was twenty I married a girl from my country who left behind all she knew to live with me on the other side of the world. She landed on a bleak spring day, and while we waited at the airport for the train home, she was dazed from the trip and couldn't stop trembling. Sadly I had no coat to offer her. My mother had insisted on lining our doorway and the building's stairs with vases full of flowers, to give my wife a traditional welcome, even though the other tenants had complained, regarding this auspicious gesture as a nuisance and even a potential hazard.

I took her here and there so she could get to know the city, going on frequent walks in a nearby park filled with trees and the occasional statue. One morning she touched the branch of an olive tree, to pluck a few of its silvery leaves, and a hideous cicada with transparent wings leaped out at her, clinging to her hand and scaring her stiff. Who knows, maybe her fear of trees developed in that moment.

A month after our wedding, my wife was pregnant, and that winter our first child was born. Still, it was a hard year. I lost my mother, who died three days after the dentist had extracted an infected tooth. And without her around, unfortunately, my brothers and I began to fight. They decided to move to different cities, different countries, even, and I couldn't afford the rent on my own. Again I found myself living in a camp, in a crowd of other people all waiting for a lucky break.

After our third child was born we applied for affordable housing. I'd always thought you needed citizenship, but my wife did a bit of research—despite her anxieties, she was a clever woman—and we realized that even people like us could claim one of those houses, as long as we had the right papers and applied through the municipal agency. Never once, as I filled out all those forms, did I expect it to actually work. But a few of the stars above us must have aligned, because we were given a home of our own, drenched in light.

OUR GOOD LUCK held out as long as it could. A few of the residents began talking among themselves in the courtyard. They banded together and started hurling derisive remarks at us whenever we left the house. Once, a couple of boys tailed our oldest son home after school, taunting him, calling us thieves and saying that we were too many. And when I went out to track those boys down, their parents said even worse things to me. I'm pretty sure they were part of the group that gathered at the gazebo along the street, with the two crisscrossing flags, where they handed out flyers to anyone who walked by, and I think they took part in a few protests, everyone with their arms stiff, outstretched at the same angle. Then one day when the seven of us were coming home, the other tenants wouldn't let us in. The women blocked the courtyard, shouting, "Pack your bags." They looked like ravens, with their dark, slick hair and thick, symmetrical eyebrows. In the end we made it past them, but the children wouldn't stop crying. At our door I expected to find some new obstacle awaiting us, one of the neighborhood bullies, maybe, but there was no one. Not even a message or symbol on our door, just the usual rickety handle.

But even inside the house, even with the windows closed, those words seeped in and began to darken our sunlit rooms, like clouds mounting in a sky on the verge of splitting open. The atmosphere grew tense and again my wife was scared to go out, not because of trees or escalators but because of those raven women and their cawing. The old widow at the end of the hall started keeping her distance, no longer inviting my wife for tea or giving candy to the kids. On the stairs, once, she cast me a sorrowful glance before hurrying off. Eventually the police and reporters got involved. Complaints were filed, and there was even a piece in the newspaper, with a photo of my frightened wife, walking past with her head down, her hands like stiff blinders shielding her eyes, while the ravens shrieked at her from all sides. Another photo showed our children at the window, stunned, staring down at the furious throng. They'd grown silent, our children, who spoke the language so well you wouldn't even think they were ours. There was a photo of the raven women, too, and a quote from one who said she was afraid of people like us.

ONE REPORTER, a young woman, came back to see us several times, wanting to help in some way. She was short, skinny, with white skin and a profusion of hair in African-style braids. She believed we had the right to live in that house, that the other tenants' behavior needed to be exposed and faced down, which was why she wanted to interview us and spread our story, presenting our point of view on the whole matter. I'd never spoken of our situation except in private with other people from my country, and the idea of sharing a little of my life with a young woman—a pretty one, I'll admit—gave me a glimmer of hope. I wanted my wife to be there, too, but in the end I went alone. It didn't sit right with her, and I don't think she trusted the reporter. A flighty woman, she remarked, though maybe she was just a little jealous. We agreed to meet in a piazza downtown, where the reporter lived. I found her waiting for me beneath a big umbrella at a round, sky-blue table, drinking iced tea and smoking one of those cigarettes you make by hand with tobacco and rolling papers. An enormous dog was asleep at her feet. She had a positive energy, and treated me almost like a friend. While I spoke, she looked up at me and took notes with her left hand, even though she was recording our conversation. At one point the reporter's cell phone rang—it was her boss, with the good news that the interview would run the next day.

I talked to her about a great many things, not just the past few months, but about the trailer where I'd spent so many hours of my childhood, about the cicadas' pulsing chorus that would accompany all my thoughts in the summer, and of course the unforgettable cicada that had landed on my wife's hand. I told her about my mother, about when she still had long black hair she could braid at night, and my father, who repaired watches but never had enough time for himself. The reporter listened patiently to everything I said, even though afterward she explained that she'd have to cut the interview down for the newspaper. Yet she'd let me carry on, and I felt relieved, even satisfied, like when I ate a sandwich after a dip in the sea, my fingers perfectly clean, my hair cool and wet. The reporter urged me to hold my ground, to not give up the apartment. Before we left, she took several photos of me sitting at that sky-blue table, and I returned home convinced that I'd saved my family and defeated the raven women. I thought that lots of people would read and appreciate our conversation, including the ones who run the city: the mayor, lawyers, and senators with power and prestige.

The next morning I went to the newsstand to buy the paper. I checked every page for my photo, but the interview wasn't there. The reporter sent me a message saying it had been pushed to the following day, that this was nothing unusual and to just be patient. But that day, too, there was no interview, nor the day after that, and she explained that a breaking global news story had forced her boss to reschedule a whole series of articles.

At home the situation worsened. There were more ravens and fewer policemen, more boys with knives in their pockets. I couldn't sleep anymore, and it was no longer the sun and birds that roused me, but that drab milky shade that hovers between darkness and day. And in that gray light, I studied my wife's face as she slept uneasily. I didn't know what to do or where to go, and it felt like the only way forward was to give up the home that had brought us such joy in the beginning, to find any other solution. One day, meanwhile, my wife took all the money we'd stashed away and bought tickets for her and the children to fly back to our country. At least there, she said, despite its many dangers, we'd never be forced to suffer such disrespect. It hurt to see them go, but I knew she was right.

I rode the train with them to the airport, and my wife told me they would stay only for a couple months, just enough time to recover, and for me to find a new place for us without everyone on my back. She was discouraged but still youthful in her long cotton dress. We checked in on the phone, when we could, my children shrunken and blurry on the screen as they waved and blew me kisses.

THE USED BOOK SALESMAN, when he heard of my situation, told me his building had a basement that might work as a hold-over, but I'd need to wait. In the meantime, thanks to a friend, I found a room in an apartment behind the central train station, shared with seven others. They were all from the same

city and spoke to each other in a language I couldn't understand. One of them did the cooking, and they ate late, around
eleven, deep pots of rice, meat, and lentils. A heavy diet I had
trouble digesting. The house was sweltering and stifling. I
slept poorly, waking up every half hour from the mosquitoes
stinging my face, ears, and eyelids, or for no good reason at all:
every night I could feel sleep abandoning me, and every morning I emerged defeated and alone in the world, without even
the shield of unconsciousness.

After the first week in that hellish apartment I called the
reporter. She asked how I was, and when I told her that my
family had left the country she was very upset and arranged
for us to meet at a coffee bar. The thought of seeing her again
lifted my spirits, but just before I got there she called back saying unfortunately we'd have to reschedule.

The coffee bar was tiny, and when I arrived the barista was
already closing up. I sat in a plastic chair along the sidewalk
and luckily he didn't say anything. He even offered me a glass
of water. I accepted, feeling a measure of peace for the first
time in a while. The street was breezy at that hour, the trees
all rustling, their thin branches curving like hooks from their
trunks. The barista swept the floor inside, a cigarette pinched
between his lips.

At one point an older gentleman arrived, wearing a light
blue shirt with short sleeves. He was hobbling a little. "They're
closing," I said to him, just as he was approaching the door. He
said nothing in return, or maybe hadn't heard me. He simply
stepped over the garbage bin the barista had placed in front of
the entrance, to keep any new customers from coming in.

"We're closed," the barista said to him.

"I'm thirsty."

"What would you like?"

"A chinotto."

The barista grabbed a glass and the little bottle, poured the chinotto, and the man drank it with his elbows propped on the counter, never setting the glass down. Then he sat in a chair beside me. I must say I was a little taken aback, and maybe even a little jealous of him, a man who felt so at home in this coffee bar, who couldn't care less about barriers, who wasn't afraid to be a nuisance. Observing him now, it dawned on me that my whole life I'd felt like an intruder or someone passing through. All this time and still I hadn't found a place of my own. Now my family, too, was gone. And in the face of those raven women, what had I done?

Just then, I swear, I had the impression that my wife was walking along the sidewalk toward the coffee bar. She wore her veil and a long cotton dress, the bottom wavering at her feet. She was pushing a stroller, and in it was a baby with a large bow at one side of her head. A boy walked in front of them, six or seven years old, staring down at his phone the whole time. I truly thought it was her. Then I thought it was a mirage. Then eventually I realized it was a different woman, a different mother, a different wife. Still, it was a miniature version of my family. I stared at her until she turned the corner. The man next to me, too, was observing her with interest. Then he said something under his breath. I couldn't hear him, and when I looked over a little perplexed, he repeated, "I said, in this heat."

"What?"

"That woman, all covered up."

I might have told him that the fabric used for those dresses is very light, that it blocks out the worst of the sun, that she resembles the noblewomen you see only in paintings in churches and museums here, just like my wife—but before I could respond, the gentleman added: "In twenty years, they'll all be that way."

I immediately walked away from the coffee bar and from that repulsive man—he, too, a raven—who in my head had insulted not only that woman but my wife. And I thought about how hard it must have been for her, walking anxiously around this city with our children, and all the thoughts and feelings of the people watching her, such a gracious and elegant creature. I understood why she'd left, and I feared she'd never return.

I WENT BACK to the apartment, but the evening was so hot that I ended up going out for a late-night stroll. I crossed the river and walked to the neighborhood of the flea market. I'd only ever been there on Sundays, when it was all blocked off to make room for the stalls. As I was walking I heard the sound of thunder, and then it started to pour, so I hid beneath an underpass and waited for it to stop. There was a wooden crate on the ground, so I took a seat. It was a clean and peaceful spot, with no one else around. Normally there'd be a constant stream of cars rushing through, but at that hour it was deserted. Two wide sidewalks lined the edges. I leaned my head back against the wall, stretched my legs out, and took a nap just like that. When I woke up it didn't feel like I'd been torn from slumber, but like I'd finally gotten a decent sleep.

. . .

THE NEXT MORNING I grabbed my few belongings and found myself a mattress and a blanket. During the day I sold a few cheap books in the underpass, nothing of any worth, but now and then someone handed over a bit of money, even some extra change so I could get a sandwich. A man came by to sweep the underpass and collect a little change for himself, and we went together to stand in line at the soup kitchen for a hot meal. Again I woke to the sound of traffic, but unlike the camps I'd stayed in, at least it was a space of my own. In some ways it felt like a big, long, narrow, palazzo, with two enormous windows on each end, always open.

Cars passed alongside me, and above me, too. If it rained, pedestrians would stop for a few minutes, waiting for the sky to clear, and no one would bother me.

Before falling asleep I'd pretend I was still in our brightly lit home, and I'd think back to the patches of light on my wife's slender foot, her thick hair splayed out over the pillow. But then I'd wince at the thought of her photo in the newspaper, her hands up like blinders by her face, and the other photo of our children at the window. From behind you couldn't see the fear in their eyes, but I remembered it. Those photos, I realized, were there in the phones of every person who walked through the underpass, and of everyone driving their cars or scooters above and below, and of all the shopkeepers around the plaza, and everyone waiting for the bus. All of them were carrying those pictures around with them, and that thought slightly subdued the pain in my chest. Then one day a man, a tourist, stopped to take a few photos of me, too, maybe thinking I was asleep, but I wasn't. What could he want with my portrait?

I got up, enraged, and tailed him for a little while. But then I let it go. No use attacking him. What would I even say? I paused for a moment in front of a shopwindow. I was very thin, my beard disheveled. And I looked lost. I wanted to buy a comb, take a shower. I didn't feel like going back into the dark of the underpass. I didn't feel like returning to the apartment with seven other people, either. And I'd be waiting for the basement forever.

WITH WHAT MONEY I had in my pocket I bought a metro ticket and rode back to the city's outskirts. I was feeling particularly nostalgic and I wanted to see the building where I'd once lived with my family, even from the outside, to catch a glimpse of the tattered awning, the hibiscus flower jutting from the balcony and dangling on its own. I missed the sharp blades of rush, the light that warmed my skin, the occasional rumble of an airplane taking off, the gulls and their frenzied cawing. I wanted to know who lived in that house now. Maybe one of the raven women, vexed by the traces we'd left behind. Had we left anything? I doubted it. Would they notice the nearly invisible marks, traced lightly in pencil behind the door, used to measure how tall our children were that spring?

I found my way to the hospital, but when I went in to take a walk among the bushes and flower beds, I was assailed by the pleasant memory of walking there with my wife, our children playing all around us. I thought I'd relax on a bench, but they were nearly all taken—just one was free, but it was missing the wooden slats where you sit, only the backrest remained. So I went on walking the streets around the hospital, until I reached, then passed, the mortuary. And there, I noticed something I'd never seen before in all the years I'd lived in this city: a swarm of moths fluttering around, dark and frantic. They moved with no destination in mind, but I didn't like them. They weren't like the white butterflies I'd seen that time over the sea.

I was feeling tired and the day had turned hot, so I stopped by a shady tree. From below, I looked up at its branches, the moss hanging in spots like little cascades, and I fell asleep with the irksome moths flitting in front of my eyes. The leaves above me trembled only faintly, and there was a kind of pollen burning my eyes. Through the gaps I could see the sky—not the vast presence that had greeted us every morning from the apartment, but a sky chewed up by the tree's foliage, jagged little pieces, each of them different.

As I contemplated those scraps of sky, I remembered the books I'd sold at the market, some of them very expensive, covered in clear plastic cases even though their pages were almost always damaged. My eyes were closed, but behind my eyelids the world was neither dark nor still, there was constant movement, a target encircled by more circles, and at one point I envisioned my wife, her eyes and cheekbones, her wonderfully curved eyebrows, even her soft smile. It was a peaceful face. More a mask than a face, really. And yet I saw her in that apparition, that mirage was mine alone. I thought of my wife and her fear of giant trees that fall and kill people out of the blue. I wanted to tell her that this tree did nothing but protect me, with no angry cicadas to leap from its leaves and cling to my hand, and that its sturdy, exposed roots were like a dark valley glimpsed from a distance.

When I woke up I wondered where to go next. The moths led my way to the train station. As I waited for the approaching train I thought only of pleasant things, and of the red and yellow poppies sprouting around my feet between the tracks.

Part II

The Steps

1 · THE MOTHER

THE MOTHER WHO climbs the steps first thing in the morning pauses when she's nearly reached the summit, turns around briefly, and admires the view. Satellite dishes and smokestacks with impetuous fumes sprout from square rooftops. Trees with flattened crowns flank the winding river; red construction cranes extend like catwalks toward nothing. She's out of breath and sweat trickles down her back.

If she manages to get there before sunrise, everything looks hazy: the buildings seem as if they're made of smoke, and a few stars linger in the gray air. Two identical cupolas are still lit up at that hour, and the faint shape of the mountains behind them resembles giant waves swelling in an ocean storm.

Today, given that she's running a little late, the sky is incandescent and the city already gleams. She goes up the last few steps, leans against one of the low stone road barriers at the top, and pulls her cell phone out of her purse to take yet another picture of the panorama. She sends it right away to her son, born this very day thirteen years ago. He'll still be at school. He lives with his grandparents on another continent, in a humid city filled with crows and palm trees and dust.

The mother can't see this immense sky when she's waiting for the bus or walking down crowded streets. It's only from here, where she is now, that she looks out at the swallows, a pair of gulls flying without moving their wings, open space stretching as far as the eye can see.

If she looks down, on the other hand, she sees the travertine steps, left sooty and filthy by the kids who gather there at night. Whole bottles, shards of bottles, cigarette butts strewn about or piled up in cracks between slabs of stone. Pried-off beer bottle caps, scattered like buttons or like clamshells along the coastline. Empty plastic cups on their sides sway from right to left like the bright beam of a lighthouse that flashes methodically over black water.

The staircase is an uneven gray, but in the middle there's a colorful section—faded by now—of alternating red and yellow, to commemorate the important victory of a beloved soccer team. Here and there, trapped in the porous stone, tiny lakes of moss and weeds.

The mother proceeds, following a long wall covered with discolored jasmine that has lost its scent. Soon she'll arrive at the building of the family she looks after six days a week.

The gate is open today and the doorman, a man who, like the mother, comes from a faraway tropical city, is doing some pruning in the garden. They say hello and remark on the plants they notice on terraces all around them, which remind them both of the vegetation where they grew up: in addition to the jasmine, there are magnolias and hibiscus, date palms and bananas, for instance.

The mother waits for the elevator while the doorman puts down his pruning shears and announces to the family that she's arrived, even though she has the key to their apartment in her purse.

She sets to work taking care of the house and two children of a husband and wife: both of them work and have various appointments in the evenings. She spends her day accompanying these children who are not her own. She takes them to school and for walks, to lessons and appointments, to the park and the dentist. The girl is five and the boy is seven. She's fond of them.

Her son was also seven when her husband, who traveled back and forth once a year, asked her to come to Rome, to help at the coffee bar he'd been running for years behind the Colosseum. Back then they were in no position to raise a son in another country. Even these days it wouldn't be easy. In any case, the years have passed and now it would be too complicated to interrupt his studies and bring him over.

While the children are at school she does the shopping. She shows the butcher the list that says how much she needs, what type of cut. Today, at the butcher, she buys some meat for her own house, too, to celebrate her son's birthday even though he won't be there.

As she runs errands she asks herself: How is my son doing, now, at this very moment? What is he up to, dressed in his uniform, sitting in a classroom or the cafeteria? What answers did he give his teachers? What is he saying under his breath to one of his classmates? Why is he laughing?

At the family's apartment, where the burners on the stove are always clean, she cooks supper. By now she's quite good at meatballs and involtini. In the afternoon she'll take the children to the park so that they can run among the marble busts of famous men. They'll walk as far as a lighthouse she finds strange, given that there's no sea below it, only more buildings, trees, ruins, and monuments.

The mother lives in a rather small apartment with her husband and several other men from their country, who all work late hours and come home bone-tired. They make deliveries on their bikes or scooters, or they peel and chop kilos of vegetables, or fry slices of eggplant in restaurant kitchens. It's her job, when she gets home, to put on the rice and red lentils and make goat stew with potatoes for the group, to set the table for seven and then clean up and do the dishes.

The father of the two children comes home in the evening, his wife is abroad at the moment. The mother lets him look over the grocery receipts and shows him the chicken, potatoes, and vegetables on the stove, everything still warm. She unties her apron and walks back to the steps that lead to the avenue where she'll catch the bus that takes her home.

The steps are no longer her own. Before she heads down, she sees two girls wearing heavy makeup, black clothes, and chunky-heeled boots, posing for photographs. Other people are sitting here and there, seemingly with nothing to do, waiting to enjoy the sunset. If there happens to be a film crew working in the middle of the staircase, with their cables and lights and dolly and clapboard, she has to stop and wait without speaking until they give the all-clear. One time she saw a famous actor, a short funny man who was pretending to fight with another guy in front of the camera.

The mother gazes once more at the sky, and in some way she feels closer to her son. She thinks: wherever one goes, the elements of the firmament—moon, sun, stars, wind, and rain—never change. Her son, as distant as he is, sees them, too.

Oddly, even though it's more arduous, she prefers climbing the steps to going down them. She's wary of the descent, she worries about losing her balance. She notices a group of boys, about her son's age, all staring into the same cell phone. They've abandoned their heavy black backpacks on the steps and they're singing a song, huddled together. She feels dizzy. She sits for a moment, setting down her plastic shopping bag.

Years ago, on Sundays, before she started working for the family, when the city emptied out, at the time of year when there seemed to be more cicadas than people, when the thrumming of those insects made it seem as if the whole world and even the air were shuddering, she and her husband would eat lunch on the steps around noon. They'd eat with their fingers, the way they'd learned, paying no attention to the passersby who might be looking at them askance. They were still a young couple, and she thought that sooner or later their son would join them. Back then she hoped they'd have another child.

She stands up and proceeds on her way. There's another couple on the steps. Tourists, lost, flushed from the heat but elegant. The wife wears a long, striped cotton sundress and a black straw hat. The husband wears a shirt with short sleeves, purple and white checks. He holds a salmon-colored map of the city in his hands.

He asks: "Where is the park?"

"Up that way," the mother replies, pointing to the summit.

The mother goes down a few steps, hesitant, and feels her head spin again. The husband with the map notices her faltering and extends an arm politely, instantly, to lend support. The husband and wife accompany the mother, who, with a mix of gratitude and embarrassment, spontaneously accepts the help of this total stranger and the surprisingly cool sensation of his skin under her hand, all the way to the bottom of the steps, where the cars are parked on a slant. For a few seconds she watches the couple climb happily up the steps, toward the park, before walking down toward the tramline and the buses.

She feels the presence of someone who's running behind her, who shouts out, grabbing onto the fabric of her skirt: "Hey, *signora!*"

She turns and sees one of the boys in the group that was listening to music. He's holding her plastic shopping bag in his hands. His forehead is covered in pimples. He says, "This is your stuff," then he rushes back to his friends sitting on the steps.

The mother thinks that the steps in this city, though made of stone, are something like the sea, where everything washes back, eventually. When she opens the shopping bag, the acrid smell of the meat she'll cook tonight rises to her nostrils.

2 · THE WIDOW

The widow who descends the steps in the late morning is scared of all the broken glass lying everywhere and is never sure where to place her feet. Her feet happen to be partially exposed because it's summer and she's wearing sandals. And what if a sliver of glass, stirred by her movements, leaps up and wedges itself under her foot the way pebbles sometimes do on certain sections of the street? Or what if it sticks briefly to the rubber sole and then falls off at home, on the floor? What if it then cuts her while she's walking barefoot around the house? When it's this hot she loves to take off her slippers and feel the cold of the marble floor. But what if the glass cuts her dog's paws? Or worse, ends up in the animal's mouth?

Long ago, the widow loved the start of summer and the ritual of going to buy a new pair of sandals for the nice weather. She always went to the same shoe store downtown— catty-corner from a mustard-colored church—that displayed the styles in the window and had only two places for customers to sit inside: a space that was more of a closet, with all the shoeboxes stacked to the ceiling. But now, the widow thinks, even that pleasure can lead to danger.

All this shattered glass is the by-product of those kids who perch on the steps like flies on a slice of melon until two or three in the morning. Some of the trampled fragments turn into sparkling dust, but other pieces are bigger, maintaining the sleek curves of the bottles they came from. Small shards, green or yellow-brown, or sometimes even a deep, cobalt blue. A few bottles remain intact, standing like sentinels on the steps. The scattered shards aren't soft and pretty like the glass the widow once collected by the sea with her mother. Each piece seemed as precious as a jewel, to be safeguarded first in her hand and then in a little velvet, silk-lined box that smelled of the sea even in winter. But these shards, dry and far from the beach, are sharp and unpleasant. All this rouses deep bitterness in her heart. Once in a while, another woman from the building will put on a pair of gloves and try to clean a bit of the nightly mess off a few steps, along with some of the rust-colored leaves that were never swept away the previous season. When it gets out of hand, a petition might circulate, but it never amounts to anything.

It's because of these kids that the widow no longer sleeps well. Before, her bedroom looked out onto the steps, and all night a lovely breeze would blow and chase the mosquitoes away. Now she sleeps in what used to be her dining room; she'd had to call two helpers over to move the furniture around. The widow lives alone, and she's in no shape to move the huge wardrobes and the table and the walnut bed she inherited from her ancestors. That localized move, from one room to another, still nags at her. She wonders if one of the men who came to help stole an antique pin, which sadly she can't find anywhere. It used to live in a little box in a drawer inside her dressing table.

Every morning the widow feels assaulted by the stream of broken bottles, the cigarette packets with their dire warnings, crushed brazenly by the teenagers and abandoned. There's often one step that's sticky with spilled beer. She feels assaulted, too, by the things people write with their spray cans on the walls that flank the steps. What does that strange, contorted language, cryptic and hideous, even mean? She's able to pick out a letter here and there—some letters look more like numbers than letters, to be honest—but never a whole word. Even though she can't make out what it says she feels insulted. It's a bit like when she hears foreigners talking on the street. Not the tourists who come to admire the neighborhood and then go away, but the others who work at the market stalls and have children and talk among themselves. The incomprehensible writing strikes her as an affront even though it's silent. It feels disrespectful. The widow notes, on the whole, a lack of respect in young people, and she thinks back to the discipline of the past, when she'd put on a uniform and sing patriotic hymns and perform exercises in the schoolyard.

Even now the widow tries to maintain a certain discipline. Every morning, for instance, she takes her dog to the park, then she goes on her own to the newsstand and afterward the coffee bar, where she drinks her espresso at a table along the sidewalk, reads the paper, and chats with her neighbors. At the bar, this morning, they were complaining about the racket from the night before. One of them filed a complaint, and in the morning he saw that the rearview mirrors on his car, parked on the street below the steps, had been smashed.

After her coffee the widow goes to the market, to buy fruits and vegetables from her favorite farm stand. She always takes the same route—she can manage, she doesn't need anyone's help, even if she's old. Some of her friends can't go out on their own anymore, they're afraid of potholes and their frail ankles and some of them even have caretakers who sleep in their homes at night, in the rooms of children who are now grown and gone. She never has her groceries delivered by some boy from another country, sent over by the owner of the farm stand in the piazza. She still likes to choose the vegetables she'll consume in the evening along with a thin slice of meat.

Before he died, her husband would place a hand on her shoulder, his arm outstretched, and together they'd perform another piece of her routine: once a day, in the late morning, she'd take her husband for a walk outside, leading him, feeling like a boat that drags a rubber raft behind it, barely skimming the surface of the water. Only her husband's feet would drag on the ground the entire time. Even now she can almost feel the weight of his hand on her shoulder, her fingers tense with worry as he aimed to put one foot in front of the other. This was the same man who, for decades before getting sick, woke up and got dressed alone and went to work and earned money and drove a car and went dancing and climbed to the most remote mountain lodges in the summer and took care of her.

Today, returning home with the groceries, she sees some carabinieri lingering in front of the gate, halfway down the steps, that leads to the back door of her building. There are three of them and she sees the word "carabinieri" written clearly in white on their shirts. The widow is both startled and relieved to see them there. In her opinion they should be patrolling the steps at all times.

When they see her they ask, "Would you open this gate for us, *signora*?"

"Did something happen?"

"We need to search the building."

"Why?"

"We think someone climbed over the gate."

The widow's heart skips a beat and she quickly takes her keys out of her purse.

"I'm sure it's one of those troublemakers who are always horsing around here until two or three in the morning."

"We fear you're right, *signora*."

"I'm always worried something like this might happen. Back in the day this was a safe, quiet part of town. I just wonder who their parents are."

"Do you have children, *signora*?"

"My husband and I, may he rest in peace, we never had children. I live with my dog."

She puts her key into the lock and opens the gate. Then she opens the door to the building. She says, "Thank you so much for coming."

"Don't mention it."

"Can I go upstairs? Is there any danger?"

"We advise you to go in without talking to anyone and to stay inside for the moment."

The carabinieri race ahead and within a few seconds they've disappeared. No one held the door open for the widow or gave her a hand with her shopping bags, the way they might have in the past. The widow expected that sort of politeness from them, but she understands that they have better things to do.

She enters her apartment, puts away the groceries, and feeds her dog. Her stomach feels unsettled. She eats very little and lies on her bed for an hour.

In the afternoon she gets ready for her usual brief stroll with the dog. She prefers to avoid the steps, so she leaves through the building's front entrance. She greets the doorman seated at the desk that also houses a row of mailboxes. She collects a few bills.

"Well then? What did the carabinieri find?"

"What carabinieri, *signora*?"

"The ones who came today. They asked me to open up, they wanted to come in, they said someone had climbed over the gate from the steps."

"How many were there?"

"There were three of them."

"All young guys?"

"I think so."

"By any chance, did you notice any carabinieri vehicles parked at the foot of the steps?"

"Not that I recall."

"What time was this?"

"Around ten or ten-thirty."

"*Signora,* I was here then, as I always am, and I wasn't aware of anything odd."

"Didn't you see them searching the building?"

"No. And unfortunately there's something fishy about what you're saying."

"What do you mean?"

"I mean, maybe they weren't really carabinieri."

"I don't follow you."

"There are people who dress up like carabinieri and convince people to let them into their buildings. Unfortunately, *signora,* they tend to take advantage of people who are, let's say, vulnerable. It's a crime ring. To be blunt, they're thieves. Otherwise they would have come here and announced themselves, don't you think? Given that I was here the whole time . . ."

"Good lord. But how is one to distinguish a real carabiniere from a fake one?"

"That I can't say for certain. But there are people up to no good everywhere. Now let me call the real carabinieri and tell them what happened."

The widow feels a spasm of terror in her veins. It's like the sensation that cuts through her groin if she steps too close to the railing of her terrace and looks down toward those happy, rowdy kids on the steps. She decides not to go to the park with her dog. She walks him in front of the building and quickly goes back home.

The following morning, when she steps out with her dog, she sees a sheet of paper taped to the front door addressed to all the residents of the condominium. It warns that there's a criminal ring moving through the neighborhood, men dressed like carabinieri who ask people to open the doors to their buildings.

Do not buzz in anyone you don't know who rings without verifying their identity.

The widow doesn't sleep well that night, not even in her relatively silent bedroom, and the following morning it's not easy to stick to her routine.

3 · THE EXPAT WIFE

The expat wife who, at lunchtime, races nimbly up the steps, is scheduled for an operation the following day. And when she's fully recovered—the doctor said that for six weeks she won't be able to lift weights or swim or go up and down the stairs—this is where she'll return, to climb these 126 steps, divided into six sections of 21, to reach the summit, where she'll feel her muscles tight behind her thighs and her knees aching and her heart pounding. Usually there's no one around at this hour, nor is there any shade, apart from a few dark patches along one side of the steps, cast down by the oleanders. At the top, awaiting her and her crazed heartbeat, there's an umbrella pine, with its languid, slanting trunk, looking like a bony sculpture by Praxiteles.

Even the low walls on both sides, covered with thin vines, have a languid, almost animalesque appearance. The lamppost up high, completely cloaked in green, really does resemble a reposing creature, a kind of green-skinned deer, with a long, straight neck and a bristly body. That boundless growth, paradoxically, reminds her of a topiary and its rigorously cultivated forms. Today, out of the corner of her eye, she notices a drying rack on the balcony with a white sheet spread over it. It looks to her like a gurney, and makes her think of the hospital, where she needs to arrive early in the morning, with an empty stomach and no nail polish.

She sees a garbageman sweeping trash up off the steps.

"Thanks so much," she tells him.

But he looks put out and complains about something, incomprehensibly, under his breath.

At the top of the staircase the expat housewife will head down the sidewalk that leads to a giant park, where—given the blazing sun at this hour—there will be very few people. In spite of the heat, she'll go for a long run to clear her head—in other words, to keep her mind off the operation and beat back the unsettling thoughts that are mounting inside her. As usual, the park will welcome her with its majestic silence. She'll run down the path, drink a little water that falls night and day in a perfectly straight stream from the bronze head of a wolf, look at the light that strikes the massive pink arch at the entrance, and, farther ahead, admire the long shadows of palms that fall on emerald fields. It's just that, today, she'll do all this with the dark premonition that she won't live to do it again.

Her solitary run through the park—past a Gothic chapel containing the mausoleum of an important family, then along a lake with ducks and geese, over a transparent bridge, and across a field where they let the grass grow longer—is usually the only way she can be outside and avoid the risk of having to talk to someone. The expat housewife prefers running alone to taking a walk downtown, where she might, perhaps, feel the urge to enter a shop, to touch this or that item for her house or try on a dress, forcing herself to converse with a salesperson or the like. Even though she's been living in Rome for several years, she has only a smattering of Italian and can keep up only to a certain point. Not like her sons, who correct her and tease her, especially the middle one, who goes to a public school, who plays and shouts out and gesticulates in the piazza as if he were born here. In the shops where they recognize her by now, and always give her a little discount, the shopkeepers talk to her anyway, telling her meandering stories she struggles to follow. Sometimes all those words cause her to lose her balance, to the point where she'll look around for something to lean on. Once—it was winter, and there was a long line because everyone wanted to buy cotechino—she feared she might have to sit down right there, on the floor of the salumeria, as the woman behind the counter explained in detail how to prepare the meat.

The expat wife's husband works for an international organization and is often in meetings on the other side of the world. Rome, for him, is a point of reference, a place to leave from and come back to. He's moved his whole family to Rome but he really doesn't live there. If anything, it's the expat housewife who's always running after their three boys. They thought at first that they'd stay for three years, but then the husband's contract was renewed and the boys made friends. And so they'd sold the pretty house in the woods outside New York that they'd bought and remodeled, with the idea of raising a family there, and with the money from the sale they bought a Roman apartment in a large palazzo, with various stairwells and a dentist and an osteopath on the ground floor and an imposing black gate that might have been a prison entrance. The expat housewife no longer has a garden like the one behind her former home, with roses the neighbors admired, nourished by heavy summer rains; nor the mossy yard where the boys would spray themselves with a hose when it was too hot; nor the patio swing where she liked to drink her coffee in the mornings and, in the evenings, glimpse the deer emerging, shy and silent, from the shrubbery. Here she has only a few pots on her terrace, plants that all tend to turn yellow and lose their leaves—she never can remember how much the person at the nursery tells her to water them—and even though she knows how to drive she doesn't feel up to dealing with the terrifying traffic along the river. She always stares in amazement at the women on their motorini, in high heels and tight skirts, blithely speeding off to wherever they go.

To be honest, the expat wife would have liked to return to the city where she grew up, where she gave birth to her children, where she still feels at ease, for tomorrow's operation, but that would have been tough to arrange. Even here it's complicated. Her husband had to cancel one of his trips so that he can stay with his family for two consecutive weeks, until she's back on her feet and can cautiously resume her daily activities. The surgeon told her they might need to remove everything. In that case, no more children and sudden menopause. The expat wife, understanding more or less—though in every interaction there's always some kernel of doubt—replied, All right, I see, though she doesn't relish the thought of losing a part of her body, in spite of the trouble it's giving her, in a city that isn't hers.

She'd wanted to say to the surgeon (though she would have lacked the words): *My diagnosis doesn't surprise me. Let me explain, Doctor. For years I've been having a dream where I need an operation. It's always the same disturbing dream, a nightmare, really. I started having it after our third son. I'm at the doctor's office, and they tell me I need an operation but they don't say why, when, or where. Every time I feel the same sense of dread because I have to tell my family I'm unwell, that I need surgery, that I have to stay in a hospital because something needs to be removed from my body. The last time I had this dream, I underwent the surgery, and when I woke up within the dream I learned that what needed to be removed was a little girl, dead, completely formed but minuscule, lodged inside me like the spare tooth buried inside my gums.*

The expat wife would rather have had that troubling, ominous dream thousands of times than undergo a real operation the next day. She's already tired from the experience of journeying from one hospital wing to another to prepare for the procedure. She's already gotten lost in the vast complex, where she first had to pay the bill and then sit in a waiting room, all alone, for more than an hour. She'd been shaken by the experience of an MRI. She'd thought, in that tight curved space, that everything would be quiet. Instead, in spite of the earplugs the radiology technician had given her, everything shook and vibrated like hundreds of tennis balls inside a dryer, which she'd use to dry the comforters at the end of winter. More than anything, she's scared, very scared, of anesthesia. Not the partial numbing at the dentist or for an epidural but total anesthesia: the complete disappearance, for a time, of any thought, dream, or sensation. To be merely a body, incapable of reacting to anything.

At the top of the steps she spots a friend of hers, an expat wife herself, who's heading down to attend a yoga class. She's carrying a backpack with a rolled-up yoga mat. The wife, who'd been climbing quickly, slows down and then stops. Her friend approaches and says:

"Ciao, it's been a while. How's it going?"

"Ciao."

"You look upset. Everything okay?"

"I'm going to have an operation," she says, and puts a hand over her belly.

"I hope it's nothing serious. I hope it all goes smoothly."

"Have you ever had an operation?"

"Once or twice, how about you?"

"Never."

"Don't worry. Do you want to come to my yoga class? It might do you good."

"I'd rather go running. Can I ask you something?"

"Sure."

"What's anesthesia like?"

"It's great."

"But what is it like to feel nothing?"

"That's just it. You don't feel anything."

"The thought upsets me."

"Don't think about it. You don't have to do anything, it just takes over."

"But what is it like?"

"It's like sleeping."

"And then?"

"Then you wake up."

"You're sure?"

"Of course. They tell you to close your eyes and think of a beautiful place or some nice memory. Let's try it. Close your eyes."

The expat housewife closes them.

"What do you see?"

She tries to see the roses in the garden of the house they've sold, the patio swing where she'd sit to drink her first cup of coffee, watching the boys, who ran on the grass and sprayed themselves with the hose when it got too hot, and the deer that stepped out from behind the shrubbery at sunset. Instead all that comes to mind is a plastic drying rack, the one she'd seen a minute ago out of the corner of her eye, that looks like a gurney. But then even that image fades, and the expat housewife senses only the sun's heat striking her back and the thundering cascade of glass bottles as the garbagemen fill up their little truck.

4 · THE GIRL

The girl who goes down the steps at two in the afternoon is surrounded by many other girls, all of whom have just been let out at the end of the school day. They descend together like a bubbling hive, or rather, like a waterfall, a live current. None of the girls invites her to join their group to get a slice of pizza or a gelato or even asks if she has a light. Unlike the others, this girl won't stop on the steps to smoke cigarettes, real or electronic, or listen to songs or look at videos on a cell phone.

They're all more or less the same age, and have the same teachers and the same homework to do in the evening. Only this girl doesn't wear the miniskirts the others wear, the ones that look like soft little lampshades, and the flouncy tops cropped just below the chest, like those curtains that cover only the top part of a window, or the tight pants and blouses and tank tops that expose a sliver of midriff, even though her stomach is always tan and perfectly flat.

The school year is nearly over and they're all sick of having to read and write and recite lines of poetry. They'd rather sit on the steps with their cell phones and study which bikinis are in style this season. Soon the other girls will leave on vacation with their families. They're already making plans for the sea, the countryside, islands, ones with volcanoes and black sand, ones without trees that once served as prisons. They have grandparents, cousins, aunts and uncles, and family friends to host them. They trade invitations—to spend ten days in the mountains or on a boat or in a farmhouse. The girl thinks: better not to get an invitation, given that her parents would never let her spend even two days, never mind ten, in the home of a family outside their community of friends.

Today is Friday and the girl won't return to the steps until Monday morning. Now she'll go straight home, to help her mother in the kitchen and look after the younger brother and sister with whom she shares a room before going to pray and then doing homework. Her classmates are already itching to get through their family dinners so that they can come back to the steps, to meet up with their closest friends and take part in the spontaneous party that will unfold with other kids from other neighborhoods. But she, she won't be parading around in a slinky dress and grabbing a drink before settling back down on the steps, to fill the night sky with laughter and secrets, intrigue and revelry. *T was looking for you tonight.*

What did he say to you? That he was looking for you. On the steps, under the handful of stars they can see, they mingle easily and instantly, sitting between the legs of boyfriends, feeling their hands around their shoulders or on the smalls of their backs. These pleasures are possible only for her classmates, whose parents probably did the same things when they were young.

The girl's parents don't typically like to spend time outside the house: eating, chatting, wandering around. They like to have dinner at home, between four walls, not out in a piazza filled with parked cars, much less on a sidewalk, with taxis and other cars and motorini and the tram and buses whizzing by. They don't have a second home anywhere. They never go to the beach to sunbathe. In fact, given that they're already tan, they prefer fair skin, the fairer the better, especially if you're a girl and have to get married one day.

The girl's father works not too far from the steps. He sells shoes, clothes, frying pans, tablecloths. Now and then he brings home some of the merchandise and her mother puts it into a big battered suitcase that lives under their bed. She says she's accumulating items for the girl's dowry and that one day they'll find her a nice husband from their community. The idea of marrying someone she doesn't know makes the girl's blood go cold, which is why she dreams of emptying that suitcase in the middle of the night while her father snores and her mother moans in her sleep. She'd put her own things into it and run away. But where to? Who would take her in? Her parents tell her that if she misbehaves—if her grades slip and if she doesn't come home to help her mother and learn how to be a good wife— they'll ship her overseas to live with relatives she's never even met, far from her classmates who have their own rooms, who lock their doors, who sleep over at each other's houses so they can trick their parents to stay out late at night and flirt with boys.

To whom might she tell the story of her only romantic experience—even though she felt it wasn't really that big of a deal? An episode linked to someone who comes from where her parents do, whom she's known since she was young and always called Uncle. In their country he'd studied chemistry, but here he worked in a pizzeria. When she was younger he'd help her with her math homework. He had a thick beard but he was young, not so tall, and he looked good in a pair of jeans and sneakers. He'd come eat with her family on Sundays and smoke alone on the balcony. Once in a while he'd ask her what something meant in Roman dialect.

This uncle was part of the group of nearly thirty people who, the previous summer, had organized a trip to a lake outside the city. They all preferred the lake to the sea because at least there was shade. They'd traveled together on a bus to spend the day eating on the grass under the trees—spicy fried foods they'd made at home, hard-boiled eggs, cutlets, chickpeas, potato chips, along with slices of watermelon. There weren't many people at the lake, maybe because the day was a bit cloudy, and the girl's younger brother and sister and cousins were happy to run around outside and play in the water with other children. Even in the shade it was still very hot, and the girl, the only teenager, wanted to go in the water. Not just up to her ankles like her mother and the other married women—some of whom were nearly her same age—who were always huddled together. But unfortunately she didn't know how to swim. The men in the group, even the older ones, had put on bathing trunks while the women stayed dressed, only rolling up their wide-legged pants so as not to soak their cotton hems.

At a certain point the chemistry-pizzeria uncle, who happened to be a good swimmer, said to the girl, who stood in the water up to her knees, "Come on in, have a nice swim." He was thin, and the material of his bathing trunks clung wrinkled to his thighs. He didn't have a big belly like her father, and down his back there was a long crease like the one between the pages of an open book. Since her mother wasn't paying attention and her father had gone for a walk along the edge of the lake, the girl followed the chemistry-pizzeria uncle until the water was up to her waist. After a brief lesson, she even put her head under water, where she glimpsed the sandy bottom and thin repeating paths like rows of snakes. "Now lie back," the uncle said. "And close your eyes." He put his hand under her back. The girl was scared, but after a few tries she felt her back suddenly curving upward, her legs meanwhile rising as if they were weightless, as if her whole body were about to levitate over the water, its rocking motion pleasantly pulling her in different directions while at the same time thrusting her toward the sky.

She came out of the water refreshed and amazed that she'd floated on her own, that she'd seen the sky from such a perspective and heard the mysterious swoosh of water in her ears. Then she saw the furious look in her mother's eyes and the embarrassment on the faces of the other women, and she realized without having to glance down that her dress was soaked and stuck to her body, nearly transparent, draped over her like the robes of certain marble statues in museums, so that everyone could see through to her nipples and the curve of her waist, the dark spot of her navel and the contours of her thighs. "Cover yourself up," her mother had hissed, handing her a towel, but then kept quiet in front of the others. After that trip to the lake the girl never saw the chemistry-pizzeria uncle again. He stopped coming over, her parents never mentioned his name, and she had no idea what became of him.

Maybe it wouldn't have been so bad to marry him, the girl thinks now as she goes down the steps: pull the dowry out from under the bed, touch the crease on his back, have a child or two, and chat with the other married women. After all, wasn't that what her classmates wanted? To find a boyfriend, a guy who sees and touches and satisfies only them? And yet her little tale—even though no one ever asks her to talk about anything of the kind—would seem strange to the other girls' ears, even absurd. And in any case, the prospect of marrying a pizza-making chemist is no longer in the cards.

As she walks down the steps she feels pleasantly pulled in different directions, as if she's floating. But instead of the water's mysterious swoosh it's the murmuring voices of other students that fill her ears. Every day, for two or three minutes, feeling at once exposed and imperceptible, she merges with the collective organism—with their arms and their smooth uncovered legs, with their loose hair—and imagines that she's one of them, without their knowing it. She drinks in their curse words and their derision, the puffs on their electronic cigarettes. They're unobtainable creatures, and so lovely; far lovelier than the boys they're all chasing after. For those few minutes she allows herself to be surrounded by their energy, their friendship, by all that marvelous white space that is their future.

The sensation lasts only so long: it's like that hesitant rain that falls briefly in summer, when you hear the crackle of drops striking leaves and rooftops and windowpanes one by one, and you run outside to feel the water for an instant on your face.

What the girl really wants is to linger awhile longer on the steps, even to stay there always, to feel like she's going down the steps with her classmates, part of a pack, transported as if she were a branch in a river, pushed forward automatically by the current. That's why she's always sorry to reach the last step, to detach from the other girls and walk along on her own.

5 · TWO BROTHERS

The two brothers sitting on the steps at sunset to drink a beer remember that, when they'd first moved to Rome with their parents, the staircase was still an out-of-the-way gathering spot. The brothers were eight and ten years old back then, but now that the younger one is fifty and the older one is fifty-two, their distant memories are either very precise or very blurred. They recall certain silly things, for example, like how the washing machine in their apartment didn't work well, so one of their first errands was to go buy socks and underwear in a tiny store run by an elderly couple, and how the woman pulled the merchandise out from a series of boxes stacked up on the shelves, as if they held currency, while the gentleman kept his eye on the flustered family, mildly suspicious, even though it would have been impossible in such a cramped store to steal or spoil or even touch anything.

The older brother remembers (still with a certain irritation) the time they waited for more than half an hour to take a bus to visit their new school—an orange building behind a tall green gate, surrounded by tennis courts and soccer fields—just to have a look, given that it was still summer and the school was closed and the place was empty.

The younger brother doesn't remember that excursion, but he does have a clear memory of the gray school bus that took them to their school filled with students from all over the world, and the flags in the courtyard, and the principal— a short, enigmatic man with an elegant but eccentric sense of style, wearing brightly colored shoes and large eyeglasses with whimsical frames—who was always seated on a bench just outside the entrance in the mornings, to welcome everyone in. And he remembered the mothers with their little handbags and jewelry and high heels (unlike their own mother with her short hair and flat shoes and no makeup and casual, forgettable clothes) who seemed ready to go out dancing at eight in the morning. They remember some of their teachers: the science teacher was also the soccer coach and made them play even when it was raining; their strict history teacher, with her pursed lips covered in fuchsia lipstick, who had taken them to Ostia and Tarquinia.

Both brothers recall the room they shared in a yellow palazzo at the foot of the steps, in a first-floor apartment that seemed frozen in time, full of dingy, uncomfortable furniture, with a deep tub in the stark white bathroom that attracted mosquitoes even in winter. If it rained in the evening they couldn't hang the wash out to dry on the roof. The primitive dryer was in even worse shape than the washer, but their mother, feeling desperate once, had turned it on and blown a fuse. All the lights went out and they had to call the landlady, who lived overseas, to find the fuse box, hidden behind an ugly still life in the hallway.

Of course they remember the girl who lived on the top floor, who was training as an opera singer and would come down to babysit, speaking Italian to them back when they hardly understood a word of it. They played card games with her and made drawings of silly creatures, folding up their sheets of paper and hiding different parts of the body—the head, the trunk, the legs up to the knees—that someone else had just drawn. The younger brother remembers holding on to those ridiculous drawings until one day they were gone.

They remember celebrating Thanksgiving in the home of another American family that had just moved from Africa. The house was freezing and filled with boxes, like a warehouse, and the mother, who was always sensitive to the cold, didn't want to take her coat off while they ate.

The younger brother remembers the lunch their mother organized, for his first birthday in Rome. The restaurant was on a piazza downtown with a big fig tree at one end. She'd invited his classmates and their parents and, even though she'd assumed no one would come, nearly everyone showed up, excited, bearing large presents, some of which were costly. The parents ate and drank at long tables; the kids were in the neighboring room of the restaurant, and they all got up to play soccer under the fig tree having barely eaten. Worried, the mother soon stepped out to call them all back in for cake.

The older brother has only a jumbled memory of that party, but he vividly recalls a fight his mother and father had—when their father booked a table at a charming trattoria, but their mother said it was just for tourists. And after dinner she stopped to sit and cry on a bench, in a piazza full of people, and the father and the two brothers were at a loss for what to do.

They move on to their memories of Sundays, when they'd climb the steps to go to the park with their father, to play baseball or soccer, and when the sun set they'd find themselves caught in a cloud of tiny insects, flitting around them on all sides. If their mother came, too, she would take a walk on her own along the gravel paths while the boys played with their father. In those days, however, she was busily at work on a book she was writing, so she often shut herself up at home to work and the brothers went out with their father (who had a few professional projects he could take care of at home without too much stress) to visit churches and museums and monuments. In general, given that their mother was often at conferences in Venice or Florence or other places, it was their father who did the shopping and made dinner. Paradoxically, it now dawns on them, their mother, who wanted so desperately to live in Rome, to do her research and write her book, was the one who seemed more often sad and on edge, while their father was mostly cheerful. He wasn't ashamed to make mistakes when he spoke Italian in restaurants and shops, but their mother would be mortified.

But now memory creeps into another crevice and the older brother insists that the man with the blond beard who joined them on trips to the countryside was driving his car when they went over toward Rieti. He, too, was a father, of twin girls who attended the same international school, but they were younger, which was why the brothers never crossed paths with them. That day there were four of them in the car; the twins weren't there. The brothers recall distinctly the details of that trip: the horses in the field who drew close to the fence, sweetly, so that they could be caressed; the amphitheater in the middle of nowhere; the bell tower with Latin inscriptions, the letters arranged vertically on their sides or upside down; and the precise rows of olive trees lining the hills. At the amphitheater the other father had been their guide, explaining how every brick had been shaped by hand, for example. Back then that sort of information made no impression on the brothers, who were busy running under the stage and leaping fearlessly from high up, toward a type of rocky landing. They were sure, as they ran wild, that the two fathers were still standing there deciphering things in Latin, but when the brothers came up to look for them they were gone. After ten minutes, they saw them emerge from behind a wall. The younger brother still believes that it was their father who'd rented a car and driven to Rieti, but the older one is convinced that they rode in the other father's beat-up Fiat.

That year had flown by. In June the brothers had to say goodbye to their teachers and to the school principal, then just after classes ended they were sent off to a camp for two weeks, to spend more time with the new friends they were about to leave behind. Their parents had taken them there and left them at the top of a mountain. Fields, cows, perilous hairpin turns. The mother had driven on the way there; more than once she failed to downshift in time on that steep terrain, and the car stalled out. There, too, unable to put the car in gear going uphill, she had started to cry.

Two weeks later the parents came back to get them. The mother looked exhausted, and when she kissed and hugged them, one of the brothers remembers her body being stiff, and she didn't exude her typical grass and lemon smell. They headed back to the city but stopped off at a certain point, just long enough to take a break and eat a sandwich. But after the sandwich they lingered a bit outside, in front of a lovely view, and that was where the father told them that he loved the other father, very much. Not just as a friend but the way he loved their mother, and that what he felt for her had evolved over the years into another type of bond. He explained that he planned to stay on in Rome and that every summer the brothers would come back to stay with him and go on nice holidays. The mother barely reacted; she looked out at the horizon and the valley in the distance as the father spoke. Now and then a train sliced through the landscape, a swift, momentary rush of noise that only intensified the silence in its wake.

And that's what happened. The boys went back with their wounded mother and picked their old life up in the university town where she taught her courses, while their father stayed behind, madly in love. Their father and the other father, who was called F, caused a stir at the orange school behind the green gate, and for a while became the main subject of the mothers' gossip. From then on the brothers had a mother in one place and two fathers in another, and they'd return to Rome every summer and take lovely holidays, touring various islands, going on a sailboat once or twice, always with F, and sometimes with his twins, who over the years had grown into two pretty girls, with hair down to their bottoms, who never paid the brothers any attention.

Eventually the father and F decided to buy a piece of land in the countryside. They had a house built there, not far from the amphitheater, initially to spend the weekends and a good part of the summer, but then every month of the year, because they wanted to pick olives and harvest grapes and take long walks in the middle of nowhere. It was a beautiful house, in a valley where the wind always kicked up after two in the afternoon and the air was thick with the smell of lavender. On the other side of the olive grove they'd built a swimming pool, which they often had to clear with a net because bees, black and white butterflies, and black lizards with white bellies and small yellow dots were always falling in. The brothers loved the place and over the years they brought their girlfriends, their wives, their children.

One afternoon, as the two o'clock wind kicked up, the father was sitting on a bench under an olive tree to admire the valley and died without suffering. F, who had gone into town to pick up a few things, found him on the grass with his eyes open toward the sky and his white hair mussed by the wind.

He was buried in the little town's cemetery, and next to him there is already a spot for F. The brothers came back for the funeral with their wives and their families. They swam in the pool with its usual host of creatures, either already dead or in the throes of dying, cleaning it again and again with the net, which became their children's favorite game.

This is why, while their wives and children are off visiting other cities, the two brothers, after seeing to some details and spending a few days with F after the funeral, have come down to Rome on their own, to visit the old neighborhood and sit on the steps from which they can still see the yellow palazzo—though it's a brighter shade of yellow these days—where they'd lived for a year with their parents when they were still husband and wife.

They carefully rehash the Sunday that they'd gone up to the

park to play with their father (who was still so young, younger than the brothers are now, his body long and lanky) while another father from their school was coming down the steps to go running along the river. The two fathers crossed paths and vaguely recognized each other; they said hello and made a date to have coffee together while the brothers clamored to get to the park. "That was the most radiant moment of my life," F had said after the funeral. In that brief exchange on the steps, both men had seen with piercing clarity what would happen, without knowing how or when. And the brothers, who love their wives and their children dearly, confess to each other that they've never felt such passion, with such certainty.

6 · THE SCREENWRITER

The screenwriter who lives at the foot of the steps, and who stays home nearly all day, is starting to feel like Dracula during this week of blazing heat. This morning, once again, the heat kept him in bed past ten. And as he'd slept, poorly, he'd heard the fitful ticking of the fan above him—now frenetic, now slow—which made him think, in his dreams, that he was young again, hunched uncomfortably over the typewriter he used to work on, its metal tentacles striking the white sheet of paper one by one.

As soon as he wakes up, he closes the shutters and turns down the slats he'd left open at night to let in a bit of air. It's already too late to take a refreshing walk. Normally, in the mornings, he likes to stroll on his own though the neighborhood, to stretch his legs and sort through his thoughts before sitting down at his desk and concentrating.

Today he sees that the sky is more white than blue. He smells something burnt in the air. A brushfire, probably, burning who knows where, in one of the city's green spaces that are more and more neglected. At lunchtime he steps out briefly, crosses the street to eat a pale, toasted sandwich at the coffee bar, and goes back home.

Caught up in a new project, the screenwriter has to spend all week in Rome. He works with another screenwriter. Normally he goes to the other's place or vice versa, and they write together in the dining room, but today it's too hot, and on top of that the taxis are on strike, so they've decided to stay put and work separately. The day before they'd had a long meeting at the director's house. They're making a film set in nineteenth-century Rome, around the time when a sixteen-year-old boy, a drummer for Garibaldi who was too short to take part in battle, was killed at the top of the staircase just above where the screenwriter usually parks his car. The film is about other things, too, but the director is determined to re-create the moment when the boy— shouting "Long live Rome!"—is shot dead in the middle of his forehead by a French soldier.

After lunch he talks to his wife—his second—who is twenty-two years younger than he is and has taken the car to the beach with their two children. His second wife can't stand summers in Rome. At the end of June, without fail, she heads off to the same sea, the same stretch of shore where she's spent every summer of her life. The same beach club, the same girlfriends under the umbrella, the same patch of sand. The house (inherited by his in-laws, a couple who, many years ago, were vaguely part of the screenwriter's social circle) is part of a cluster of condos, with a gate that shuts out the world and a private pedestrian tunnel for residents that leads directly to the sea. His wife spends her days chatting with friends she grew up with, maybe bumping into an ex-boyfriend or two at the coffee bar, and if she has to run back to the house, for whatever reason, she leaves her towel and creams nonchalantly on the sand. The door to their condo is always open, the kids running from place to place, forming groups according to age to play cops and robbers. Bougainvillea, sticky sand, skinny lizards that leap around your feet. A paradise where the sun sizzles on the water at sunset—a place where the screenwriter never gets any work done.

These past few days the screenwriter has been going out every night for dinner, either on his own or with a friend, and then to study the faces of young people, to remember what a sixteen-year-old looks and acts like, his attitude, how he carries himself. Some of them are already men, others still children. They're all blessed, and cursed, trapped in this boiling hot city, as opposed to his own young children, off swimming peacefully in the sea beloved by their mother and grandparents and great-grandparents, running free until midnight behind the gate that shuts out the world. The children he's had with his second wife are still a ways from puberty: the girl, all skin and bone, wears only the bottom of her bikini when she goes in the water; and the boy wants nothing to do with girls. But they'll change soon enough. And they'll come to resemble the screenwriter's other two children, from his first marriage, who are now grown up and have children of their own.

At night the steps turn into a kind of ancient amphitheater, with groups of teenagers seated out in the open, waiting to watch some tragedy unfold. Except they themselves are the spectacle: the nightly drama lies in their exchanges, intense or completely casual, private even though they're in public. They pay attention to nothing but the cliques around them. What do they know of the poor drummer boy, sacrificed at the top of the steps back in Garibaldi's day? Studying them one night, the screenwriter had been struck by a thought: What would it be like to film this scene, this nightly ritual? To make a movie about it, a documentary, perhaps, following the lives of a few of these kids, with the steps as a backdrop? What would it be like to interview them, to inch closer to their skittish, unknowable spirits? But after that initial spark he'd set the idea aside. He doesn't want to spend his time thinking about their presence, which is only a nuisance, in the end.

In the evening he stops working and closes the cover of his hot, humming laptop. He takes a shower, shaves, combs his hair. He puts on a fresh linen shirt and slips a watch (a present from his second wife, at a surprise party for his sixtieth birthday) around his wrist so that he can calculate the length of his walk. He packs a (small) suitcase to take with him to the beach the next day. The friend he was planning to join for a spritz on a hotel rooftop calls at the last minute to say he can't make it. So the screenwriter stays home, drinks a glass of grapefruit juice, and watches something on television.

Around nine o'clock he goes to dinner on his own, to a neighborhood trattoria, at the end of a street leading to a big peach-colored church that sits on an angle from the restaurant. The smell of something burning in the air has faded, though there's still a trace of it. He greets the owners—a mother and son—and takes a table outside, a spot that allows him to admire the church's façade set against the sky, which at the moment is a vivid shade of cobalt. The usual waiter brings him a first course, then a second, with white wine. He eats, then accepts some amaro in a small, pleasantly frosty glass. All the while admiring the empty, peach-colored church. Only now it's turned the dark pink shade of a watermelon.

As he drinks his amaro, a wasp comes to visit, briefly tasting the cantuccio left on his plate. It's typically at lunch, the screenwriter thinks to himself, that the wasps are a bother. Must be the still air. His thoughts drift back to a vacation from decades earlier, when he was married to his first wife, and the kids were small, and he and his wife still got along. They were on an island in Greece. And every morning they ate breakfast outdoors at a table facing the sea, under a billowing white cotton tent, a table large enough to seat all the guests at the hotel. A long and luxurious breakfast, with bread and fresh-baked sesame cookies and thick, delicious yogurt with honey and fresh fruit from the island. But there was no breeze to speak of, alas, and the wasps were always a bother. They came zigzagging and careening dangerously close, skimming the arms and cheeks and bare shoulders of their children, terrorizing them. Their boy would freeze up and their girl, wide-eyed, would burst into tears.

There was no use trying to chase them away. Instead the screenwriter made use of the empty glasses on the table, turning them swiftly upside down to trap the wasps. He'd become an expert, using two glasses at the same time, one in each hand. And once they were trapped, the wasps turned into a source of entertainment for his children, who studied them, fascinated. By the end of breakfast, there were always at least six or seven glasses flipped over on the table, the wasps hovering around inside their cylindrical glass prisons. Rapidly they'd shuttle up and down, searching for a way out, on their delicate, V-shaped wings. Some would fall to the table, but they didn't suffocate, they never stopped moving, they were never at rest. No, they were constantly feverish, determined, disagreeable. He noticed that whenever he trapped a wasp, another would arrive to replace it, perhaps the result of some chemical form of communication within their colonies. Before leaving the table, to go for a swim in the pool or the sea, the screenwriter would free the whole lot of them. And as soon as he lifted the glasses, the creatures would burst from their enclosures and dart away, even more determined, up toward the clouds.

The screenwriter doubts that his adult children remember anything about that summer, now, and about the wasps their father trapped inside glasses when he was still a hero to them. He seizes a glass, tosses the water out, and tries trapping the wasp in front of him. To no avail.

After dinner he goes walking along the uneven streets. He avoids the Lungotevere, the piazzas full of people. Still feeling like a version of Dracula, who emerges only at night, he drinks in the splendor of his city, even if it's a splendor under siege and always in decline. Unlike his wife, he loves and forgives Rome in every season. He walks unrelentingly, in search of a breeze. He reads the commemorative plaques mounted on buildings in deserted corners, the Jewish names etched in gold among the sampietrini, at the foot of certain doorways. He stops at a fountain ignored by tourists at this hour. Finally, around eleven o'clock, it feels nice to be out. The burnt smell in the air has dissipated entirely. He walks for over an hour through the emptier and emptier city, checking his watch now and then. He'll sleep well tonight, he thinks. Satisfied, he heads back to his apartment.

Tomorrow morning he'll take the train to join his second family. His wife will come pick him up at the station in their car and he'll be overjoyed to see her. At forty-two, she still looks like one of the girls worthy of sitting on the staircase in the evening. They'll take a walk along the shore, toward a tower on a promontory, and say hello to various friends (and maybe a few of his wife's ex-boyfriends) on the beach. And he'll think, with a certain melancholy, when he watches the water clamber up the shore, that every effort, and even every pleasure in life, every goal that's reached and achieved, every recollection, lasts only for an instant, just like the water that throws itself onto the beach, leaving a spontaneous imprint whose wavering contours, like the line drawn by a heart monitor, are never quite the same.

The screenwriter, almost back at his apartment, turns the corner expecting the usual boisterous amphitheater. Instead he sees that the steps are empty; tonight, for whatever reason, the neighborhood kids have decided to make a ruckus elsewhere. He notices the white dots of light from the lampposts, creating a kind of symmetrical constellation around the staircase, like a big, wide letter M; and the six low road barriers at the top, lined up in a row. He wonders if a car has ever skidded off the road up there, and tumbled down.

He continues up his street, which is silent now and much darker, walking past cars parked on a slant. He's nearly at the door to his building when he decides, at the last minute, to walk up the steps, all 126 of them. Just to do it, because tonight the staircase is all his, and because he feels like exerting himself one last time before collapsing into bed under the ticking ceiling fan.

After the first set of steps he becomes aware of a presence nearby. More than one person—at least two, maybe three. Then he feels an object at the back of his neck, something sharp, but thicker than a knife, not long enough to be a knife. He hears the voice of a boy who's been drinking. "Give us all your money. And the watch."

He now realizes that the cold, delicate object pressed to his neck is most certainly a shard of glass, one of the many at his feet, and he knows that, at this hour, he has no choice other than to cooperate. He takes out his wallet, hands over the cash; as soon as he extends his arm, a kid snatches the watch his wife gave him at his surprise party. Before turning around, he puts a hand on his neck to check if there's blood. His fingers are clean. He feels only a stinging sensation. And with his eyes, for as long as he can, he follows the shapes of the three kids who—like the wasps he'd once so deftly caught and released, to protect his children—dart away and disappear.

Part III

The Delivery

A PACKAGE ARRIVES while the *signora* is on vacation, sent from overseas. But there's a fee to pay on delivery, so the postman leaves a message with the doorman. It says the package is being held at the post office. When I stop in one day to water the plants, I set the slip of paper aside. It looks like a postcard. I put it on the bookcase along with the bills and other things that look important.

The *signora* is spending time in the countryside, staying with friends. She'll be back at the end of the month, when the weather turns cooler.

But after a week she calls and says she's already returned to the city.

She tells me she was walking across the lawn in the dark when she fell into a hole and sprained her ankle. She thinks it was probably the den of some sort of animal. Fortunately, the evening after her accident, there was a doctor among the dinner guests. He told her she needed to be in the city for a scan and that she'd likely need physical therapy.

She couldn't drive, so the son of the family that was hosting her drove her car home, then went straight back to the countryside on the train.

"To be honest, it's a blessing," the *signora* says as I help unpack her suitcase. "I slept horribly up there, I kept having nightmares. I'd get up every night at three o'clock and stay awake."

But I don't think she's pleased to be back. She seems disappointed to be stuck on the couch all the time. She can't manage the steps that lead to her bed in the loft space, where she likes to sleep—a little den of her own—surrounded by her costume jewelry: colored beads that hang thickly on the wall, fat shiny bangles organized on a shelf.

The *signora* is an architect. She isn't that old even though the skin above her cheekbones is creased like dried figs. She tends to work from home, but she's an active woman, always hosting dinners, inviting a dozen people over, and she travels frequently here and there. I come by a few times a week to do the laundry and tidy up.

She's been to my country a number of times, so now and again we strike up a conversation. She travels there in the winter, to a town along the coast I've never seen.

She goes to visit temples and cleanse her system of toxins. She follows strange diets. For example, she once had to drink a lot of lemon juice.

When she comes back her skin is tanned and she's thinner, more energetic. She tells me that she loves the textiles and the colors of the buildings and the way the women move their bodies. She shows me pictures on her cell phone of the ruddy dirt roads, the white sandy beaches.

The *signora* lives alone. Once she lived in a different apartment with a husband and two children.

The son is studying to become an engineer and the daughter moved away to be close to her boyfriend. They both live overseas, in different countries.

The father of her children, an academic who talks on television sometimes, married a woman three years older than their daughter. That's what she tells me.

The *signora* can't go out now, she needs to rest her ankle, so I come by every morning with groceries and stay all day.

The *signora* always likes to accomplish things, so now that she's recovering from her sprain she'd like to tackle a few projects around the house. I don't mind helping.

For instance, she asks me to empty out some of her closets and throw their contents onto the bed, the sofas, and the floor. I've inherited some of her clothing as a result.

At first I hesitated, given that her skirts and dresses all end at the knee and I'm used to longer garments. But she insisted: "Enough with covering yourself from top to bottom. It's so hot, you've got great legs, no one will mention it here. You'll feel much better in these."

One day she asks me to hand her all the mail I'd set aside and she discovers the notice about the package at the post office.

"Who knows what it is. Probably a book. Or maybe one of the kids sent me something. Stop by the post office and pick it up for me."

And she signs the card, authorizing me to go in her place.

IT'S SO HOT, I don't feel up to crossing the bridge on foot at this hour. The sun's beating down. I take the bus instead. But the bus gets on my nerves. It rattles like a drill that's about to split the sidewalk in two.

Sitting down is no better. The seats are uncomfortable, and they're so high that my feet barely touch the floor.

Standing in that unfriendly crowd, I never feel at ease.

On the other hand, I like this polka-dot skirt the *signora* gave me, with two deep pockets and soft pleats. The fabric is dark blue and the small dots are white. I haven't worn something like this since I was a schoolgirl.

The post office is crowded. I take a number and wait.

The wooden seats are attached to a bar that's anchored to the marble floor.

I look at the windows and the red numbers on the screen that change from time to time. When they change there's a buzzing sound, and the new number flashes.

The employees, all of them women, sit behind the windows and chat with one another like aunts at a wedding.

The rest of us sit silent, like members of a small audience watching a performance.

On the upper level there's even a sort of balcony. It's curved and made of glass.

All told, things could be worse. It's a chaotic place but at least it's cool.

A man next to me is reading the newspaper. And out of the corner of my eye, on the front page, I see a photograph. I learn, from the headline, that it was taken in a village close to my city, where it rains a great deal in summer.

Here, on the other hand, all summer, it hasn't rained. People say that they're going to shut off the city drinking fountains that flow day and night.

The photograph shows a row of bodies. All of them children. They were crossing a river at the border when they drowned. In the photograph, two mothers cover the bodies with an enormous tarp as if to keep them warm while they sleep. The children lie facing the sky. But then I notice that one of them, a small boy, has turned his head to the left, eyes closed as if he's just dozed off.

I wait for about half an hour before my number appears on the screen. I walk up to the window but I still need to wait, because the girl in front of me, who appeared to be finished, lingers, talking to the woman there. She's got a few more questions. Her transparent dress exposes her black bra and nearly the full length of her legs. Her shoulders are bare and she wears flat sandals. But like the *signora* told me, no one mentions it here. One of the thin straps of her dress has fallen from her shoulder, but she doesn't seem to care. She never bothers to adjust it. She's still talking with the woman behind the window. They have so much to say to each other, it's as if they're friends.

The employee was smiling while she spoke to the girl but her smile disappears when it's my turn at the window.

I pull out the card signed by the *signora,* and my identity card.

But the employee says, briskly, "We're not holding this anymore. The package has been sent back."

Then she points out clearly, with the edge of her fingernail, the part where it says that the package was only going to be held for seven business days from the day the notice was left.

"Where was it sent back to?"

"I wouldn't know."

"Who sent it?"

"I have no idea."

"And now what?"

"Now I help the next person in line, *arrivederci*."

I feel terrible and hope the *signora* won't be too angry. There's finally a bit of a breeze outside so I decide to walk back. It's lovely to feel the skirt billowing around me like a cloud as I cross the bridge.

I stop on the bridge for a moment to look at the river that always flows more quickly than I expect. The river is green, as are all the plants and the giant leaves of the plane trees lining the banks. On the wall, just by my elbow, I notice a mass of ants. They're scattered but clustered. They're transporting a dead fly much larger and heavier than they are. Their determination always moves me.

And as usual I notice a young couple slowly kissing, without a care, ensconced in their own world. He's standing. She's seated calmly, daringly, on the parapet. A light push, perhaps even a gust of wind, would be enough to send her backwards over the edge.

After crossing the bridge, I walk beneath a derelict archway sprouting weeds.

I proceed past a series of shops that all sell bicycles. Suddenly I feel the urge to ride one, to go down to the river's edge and pedal along the path.

I can't remember the last time I rode a bicycle. Do I still know how? I learned when I was a girl, my brother taught me. We'd go exploring wide, dusty dirt roads together. I still recall the pleasure of the breeze against my face.

Instead I keep walking toward the *signora*'s house, in the cool green shade, along a quiet street with only a few cars on it.

I think, What a pity about the package. I should have gone

right away to pick it up. I'm absorbed in various thoughts when I hear a motorino behind me.

It's quite close and seems to slow down when a voice calls out, "Go wash those dirty legs."

I turn my head and for a second I see them. There are two boys on the motorino. They wear helmets and sunglasses with thin frames. Then I feel tremendous pain in my shoulder, and I see the sky overhead.

We've decided to go back to the same beach as last time. Maybe those same girls will be hanging out at the bar. I'd liked the one with the blue nail polish, the tattoos running down her arm. We'd talked for a few minutes. Maybe I'll bump into her again.

To leave the city we take a road with walls on both sides. It's like a long thin ribbon. We climb uphill and coast down. Then we ride through the countryside. It's pretty, with the sea spreading out to the left. Now the ground is so flat that we can see a lot of sky, with big white clouds that sit low over the landscape.

The highway is smooth and dark. The asphalt looks brand-new, it's as if we're the first people to ever travel on it.

At one point we pass by a city perched high on a hill, and I remember something my grandfather once told me when I was little: that a long time ago the sea came right up to that city, before this road existed.

It's past four when we get to the beach. It's still hot and everything looks parched. People say it hasn't rained for over a hundred days. The parking lot is full of dust and we can hear all the insects teeming in the brush.

While my friend parks his motorino, I see a guy pushing a wheelchair. Another guy is sitting in it, maybe his brother. Their faces look alike but the legs of the one in the wheelchair are deformed. They're too short and taper off at the ends.

I take off my shoes. All I want is to get into the water, but my friend bumps into someone he knows so we stop at the bar and have a coffee.

While they're talking I feel something bothering me, something at my feet, and when I look down I see that they're covered with ants, crawling rapidly and without direction. My friend wants to eat something but I'm not hungry. He has a sandwich and a glass of water. He looks down at his plate as he eats. Finally we head to the beach. I leave my friend on the sand—even though the air is oppressive, he says he feels cold and lies facedown in the sun.

The water is full of people, kids, women talking to one another. Along the shore a father calls in vain for his son: Fede, Federico, Fe-de-rì!

More of those low clouds surround me, it's like they're sitting on top of the dunes. The water is a little muddy but it's refreshing, it's just that I feel a little tense.

I float and look at all the people in the water, and at the separate beach clubs along the sand.

Looking at the sky, so blue and clear overhead, calms me more than the crowded water.

I swim for a while, then get out and take a walk.

I see some guys zigzagging between groups of sunbathers. They're selling hats, towels, and cotton skirts. They go up to one beach chair after another, approaching women who are half-asleep, a bit annoyed by them, a bit curious.

One of the men has a row of purses hanging from his fore-arm, as if they were empty hangers hooked over a closet rod. When I edge closer, I spy an arm covered with tattoos. It's her, she's with the same friend.

I linger and watch the guy crouch over their beach blanket, talking up his merchandise, draping the items over their legs in a cocky way. He's selling scarves in a bunch of different colors, at least a dozen. They look soft, nearly see-through.

The girls chat with him. They're impressed, undecided. They're tempted.

The guy looks like the others who have moved into my family's part of the city. Once it was a quiet neighborhood between the train tracks and an aqueduct built by an emperor.

They have their own little grocery stores. They put signs in their windows that my family can't read. They pray barefoot in squalid buildings. Their kids play soccer on the other side of the aqueduct, on a dry patch of ground.

My parents complain that before long, they'll outnumber us. Meanwhile the bar my friend's parents own isn't making enough money because, he says, people from that part of the world don't crowd the counter in the mornings or after lunch; they don't even like our coffee.

The guy selling bags and scarves has been hanging around the girls for way too long. Why don't they just tell him to get lost?

I'd say something but I shouldn't draw attention to myself right now. The girls are smiling and laughing, they're pulling money out of their wallets, they're buying this and that.

"What's your name?" the one with the tattoos asks him. She hasn't glanced once in my direction.

I start sweating so much I get back into the water.

I stay in until the sun starts to set and the bodies of everyone on the beach start to turn that same glowing gold.

I dive down a few times to try to touch the bottom. There's not much to see. Just a few drab-looking fish wandering around. A few twisted-up branches.

Nothing shiny like the pistol my friend tossed from his motorino into the river.

He'd fired twice and she'd fallen to the ground. She had a long dark braid with a thick, bright red hair tie at the bottom. She was short and wore a polka-dot skirt.

I'd said, "Fuck, you really shot her."

But my friend didn't reply, he just sped up.

I'd hollered, "You said you weren't going to aim at anyone!" I'd added, "She was a *ragazza*."

My friend waited to toss the gun before saying, "It's only to scare them, it's not like she'll die from it."

But now I'm scared. I don't feel the adrenaline of those nights we cruise around drunk with markers, writing messages on walls or on the backs of street signs.

As the sun keeps sinking into the sea, the lifeguard working at the neighboring beach club starts closing up the umbrellas. They're all red, just like the hair tie at the bottom of the young woman's braid. And once they're closed up and bound tight, they remind me of her long braid, too. But the skirt, while she was walking, was light and flowing around her dark legs.

I swim a little more but now I'm getting cold, and I don't like being the only person left in the water—there's only one other guy out swimming, farther from shore.

I wonder if someone saw us on the street with all the bicycle shops. Maybe someone remembers me yelling those words at her, to insult her.

I come out of the water. I don't have a towel, and by now the guys who sell them have left.

I'm tired but I'm not happy like the others, baked from the sun, walking toward the parking lot to go home.

As I wait to dry off, the waves hiss in my ears like snakes.

I find my friend, who tells me that he took a nap and that it's time to go. He complains that his shoulders got too much sun.

As we ride back to the city, I notice that the back of my friend's neck got a little burned, too. There's a mix of white clouds and dark ones. All of them are huge and low, like smoke billowing up from a fire under the horizon. A stream of cold air pelts my face on the ride.

When we notice a cop car gaining speed my friend slows down a little and I glance back out of instinct.

No one stops us. They're after someone else up ahead.

The sky above us is pale and that thin crescent moon has been there all day.

At the hospital they tell me they'd fired from about ten meters away and that I'd fainted. A man passing by on his bicycle had called for an ambulance.

They're taking care of me in the emergency room. In the end they don't need to admit me. They've found the pellets, they explain that they were fired by an air pistol. They send me home with two big X-rays that show the pellets scattered through my body. They look like a series of lights in a town seen from a hilltop at night, or the little dots on the *signora*'s skirt.

I need to recover now, just like the *signora*. I can't work for her until I'm better. She tells me to take all the time I need. To be honest, I'm glad I don't have to spend time in her house, where I'd probably end up thinking too much about the afternoon I went to the post office, to pick up the package that had already been returned to its sender.

One of my cousins is helping the *signora* now, while I work for another cousin who has a store that sells bottles of beer, cereal, cases of water, and toilet paper until two in the morning. I run the cash register. As long as I sit still, I can manage.

My cousin tells me I was lucky, that wounds like mine will eventually heal. He knows someone who was beaten up waiting at a bus stop one night and lost his eye.

He discourages me from filing a report. In his opinion it's better not to get mixed up with the police.

They were young, that's all I took in. Maybe they were friends who had nothing better to do, like the teenagers who turn up around eleven at night to buy beer and smoke in front of the convenience store.

These kids don't bother me. They chat late into the night, in the dark, seated on the two steps outside the store or leaning against a parked car. They're like cats or insects that come out only at night, that meet up and colonize the edges of the streets. They prowl in the dark, fueled by lust. I hear their voices, their secret exchanges, but all the words meld together. I hear occasional laughter and the venting of fumbling, precocious desires that sail up, weightless, to the stars.

When I was their age I did more or less the same, I'd stop

with my friends after school on a certain street, a spot where students would gather.

We'd flaunt ourselves to the world and have something to eat. I remember one boy, skinny, who was already in college, studying physics. He'd single me out with his eyes. He once bought me something to drink.

But I left that world behind. Wanting more out of life, I came here willingly.

Sometimes I catch sight of a particular kind of face: full pale lips, shiny skin, the expression lit up by the heavy shaft of light from a lamppost.

For a few hours after midnight, this ancient city seems to belong only to the young: a joyful kingdom, ephemeral, all their own.

Among them, I notice a few kids with different features, with darker complexions like mine. A strange harmony binds them together: nocturnal complicity, identical gestures.

I like watching them chat with each other, scattered but gathered from all around. They'll never know that their presence soothes me, even though, at the same time, I feel a pain in the center of my chest, as if one of those pellets were lodged in my heart, and I nearly die from envy.

The Procession

· 1 ·

THE JET LAG DOESN'T bother her. If anything, that sharp
blade of light cutting through the window of the plane
as they'd landed, turning their nocturnal flight into sudden
dawn, had startled her like an electric charge. On the train
they took from the airport (each of them had only one suitcase, one backpack, as if they were a young couple touring
the world) she recognized the sky, the fields, the giant reeds, a
few cupolas here and there. Yellow buildings in the distance,
balconies loaded with plants. From the tram, she saw the same
plane trees lining the avenue, with thick trunks and bark like a
soldier's camouflage. This morning she got up early, to enjoy
her breakfast alone and pick up a few things in the nearby
piazza.

He's still groggy, he's slept till noon. He's never been to
Rome, though he's been to a few other European capitals.
They're here to celebrate his wife's fiftieth birthday, though
she really turned fifty a few months ago, while they were busy

working at the university where they both teach. He teaches law, she teaches biology. He knows that Rome is part of her past. That long before they met, when she was nineteen, she'd studied there for a year and fallen in love for the first time, with a Roman boy.

The apartment they've rented has clashing furnishings. The small leather couch and stainless-steel lamps are distinctly modern, as is the glass coffee table. But they're paired with huge, gilt-framed mirrors, a corner china cabinet with three squat legs, and a semicircular console furnished with one leg only, curving down the front like the tail of a wild animal. On the coffee table, a vase of sunflowers have just begun to droop. Against one of the walls, there's a piano with chipped, yellowed keys, on top of which sits a series of small, dark landscape paintings.

The room next door has a huge cupboard for all the crockery, and a big round dining table with grotesques carved into its edges and various objects scattered on top: books, notebooks, magazines, water bottles, electronic devices, cords, packs of crackers, a camera, sunglasses, tubes of ointments, mosquito spray, and a bottle of pills. A crystal chandelier droops over the table. It's missing some of its candles, and the escutcheon is partly detached from the ceiling.

He's sitting on the sofa, tying the laces on a pair of sneakers. He's just taken a shower and his hair is still wet. She's ready to go. Her purse is strapped across her shoulder, she wears a long linen dress. Her silver hair, parted in the middle, is gathered at her neck. As she waits for her husband in front of the piano, she rummages through a bowl filled with keys.

"I can't get it to open."

"What?"

"The room at the end of the hallway. It's locked."

"I thought that was a closet."

"No, I saw it from outside this morning when I left. It's the room on the corner of the building. I bet it gets the best light at this time of day."

"Is it already hot out?"

"A bit, but it's not humid. Did you eat?"

"I found some bread in the kitchen."

"I brought you a cornetto, didn't you see it?"

She goes to the kitchen and brings back a small white paper bag.

"Here, it's still warm."

She opens the piano bench in front of the instrument and pulls out some lesson books. She sits on the bench and says, "There's an amazing spot in the hallway, have you noticed? Where a magical breeze passes through, it's like being by the sea."

He swallows and says, "Everything feels like the sea here. I didn't expect so many seagulls. Speaking of breezes, we should put some sort of weight in front of the French doors off the kitchen. They slam when the wind blows."

"Did you see that there's a washing machine on the balcony?"

"There's an old dishwasher, too."

"Who knows what's inside it."

"Inside the dishwasher?"

"No, inside that locked room."

"Probably the landlady's stuff. All the nice things she hides away so that her tenants don't destroy the place."

She strikes a random piano key, which emits no sound. "Was this the apartment where they didn't allow children?"

"No, that was the pricey penthouse on the Tiber."

"It would be ideal to use that locked room as a study."

"We can both work at the dining table, it's huge."

She looks up at the ceiling.

"See how it's starting to detach? You don't think the chandelier could come crashing down, do you?"

"That metal piece is only decorative."

"To me it doesn't look like it's attached to anything. How's your cornetto?"

"Good. What's in it?"

"Visciola."

"What's that?"

"It's sort of like cherry, but it's something else."

"Did you have the same thing?"

"I did. I sat at a table at the coffee bar and tried to read a few headlines in the newspaper."

"Tomorrow we can go together."

"Tomorrow's Sunday and the coffee bar is closed."

"Oh."

"So, are we ready? Let's go, if not we'll miss the procession."

He leans his head against the back of the couch and closes his eyes.

"And what if we stayed here to avoid the heat and enjoyed the magical breeze in the apartment?"

"Come on, it's something worth seeing."

"Explain one more time what it's all about?"

"The Virgin goes by."

"It's not like you're a believer."

"That's not the point. I'd like to see her again, after all these years. That's the reason I looked for a place to stay in this neighborhood."

"Really?"

"I still remember her so vividly."

"Who?"

"The Virgin."

"What's she like?"

"She's beautiful. Carved in wood and wrapped in a silk gown, wearing precious jewels. Men dressed in white carry her in on their shoulders. First the band plays, then you see the palanquin raised high and all the believers recite the rosary. The crowd tosses rose petals at her."

"And what's it all supposed to mean?"

"The first one was held to commemorate the end of some sort of disaster, a bad storm or an earthquake, a plague, maybe, I don't remember anymore. They've been doing it for ages now, and they always make the same stops. I thought it was so moving. An authentic piece of the city. You won't find that in any museum."

"You think it will be just like it was thirty years ago?"

"I'm sure of it. The fruit vendor told me the procession has always been the same and that he's looked forward to it every year since he was born, that he hasn't missed a single one."

"I don't think there's anything I've done the exact same way every year of my life."

"Here the same things happen, again and again."

He opens the front door. "Do we have the keys?"

"Yes, they're in my purse, and there's a second set in that bowl."

"Should we call for the elevator?"

"I'd rather take the stairs."

"But we're on the top floor."

"What if it gets stuck? It's July and the building is practically empty. I like taking the stairs, there's always a nice breeze blowing through the stairwell."

· 2 ·

They arrive at a triangular piazza built on a moderate incline. This space, too, feels like a living room of sorts, with streets branching off of it here and there like hallways. There's nothing noteworthy at the center, no fountain or statue that serves as a point of reference. Just a playground. The façades of the buildings—all of them five or six stories tall—are painted in warm colors: yellow, pink, orange. They have huge front doors and windows with green or brown shutters. Some have narrow balconies on the top floor with potted plants that overlook the piazza, which is surrounded by three coffee bars, a pharmacy, a hardware store, a bakery, a wine bar, a framer, and various other shops and restaurants. A few benches and trees run along the sides. Along one side, up a few steps, there's a structure that houses a collection of permanent market stalls. The only truly historical element, at a slight remove from the gravitational center of the piazza, is the entrance to a small medieval church made of bricks. Some of the bricks are missing. The entrance is flanked by two columns—one smooth and the other grooved—that are two different shades of gray.

The couple stops briefly in front of the wrought-iron gate

of the church, then moves on. It's past two in the afternoon and there are only a handful of people walking around. The stores and market stalls are closed, but children play soccer or ride their bicycles. A group of elderly people sit on a bench, and a few faces stare out from the windows of the buildings.

The husband and wife walk slowly through the space.

"Where should we wait?" he asks.

"You decide."

"Which way does the procession come?"

"It should come down that way."

"But there's no one here. Did we get the time wrong?"

"The fruit vendor said it would start around three and to get here a little early."

"Maybe you misunderstood."

"I didn't misunderstand."

A soccer ball rolls toward the couple's feet. He stops it and kicks it back toward the children.

"There's some shade over that way."

They settle along a low wall, leaning against it without sitting down. They have their backs to the piazza. The husband rolls up his sleeves.

"You said it wasn't humid today."

"It was better in the morning, in the shade."

Two minutes go by. He looks at his cell phone and takes a few pictures. She follows the children playing soccer with her eyes and he looks up at the faces of the older people framed by their windows. He says:

"They have the best view."

"Who?"

"The people in the windows."

"It's odd."

"What's odd?"

"They just seem so small in those windows, each of them fixed in their own dark square. And see how they always stand to one side, never at the center?"

"You think they're looking at us?"

"I think they've seen enough tourists by now."

"But when will the Virgin go by?"

"Be patient. We need to wait."

"Should we go get something to eat?"

"You just ate."

"It was only a cornetto. Should we have lunch and come back?"

"If we have lunch now we won't be hungry at eight. I booked us a table at a restaurant that's always full."

"Should we get a gelato then?"

"Maybe later, if you want. There's a good gelateria on the other side of the avenue."

"Has the piazza changed much?"

"The playground wasn't here."

After a moment the husband asks: "Were you with him when you saw the procession for the first time?"

"Who?"

"The guy you were seeing."

"We were together, but that day he was busy, so I took a walk by myself. It was amazing, I'd crossed the river and then I got completely lost. In those days, without cell phones, you'd get lost all the time in Rome. So I stumbled upon the procession by total chance."

"Is he on your mind, now that you're here?"

"We dated for three months."

"Why don't you get in touch?"

"It was ages ago."

"I wouldn't mind meeting the first love of your life."

"I want to be here with you."

As they hold hands, two women, about the same age as the wife, cross the piazza together arm in arm. It's hard to tell if they're friends or lovers or sisters. They stride along swiftly, then slip down a side street and vanish. Other women appear, either alone or with children or companions. Mothers with daughters. More and more arrive, chatting and laughing and filling up the piazza. Their hair and the hems of their skirts seem like living things, extending like tentacles from their heads and clothing.

"They have so much to say," he observes.

"And it always seems so urgent."

"What are they telling each other? Can you understand?"

"I can only catch a few words."

"It's as if they're all friends."

"They're all so stunning."

"You're stunning, too."

"Not like these women."

"What makes you any different?"

"When I watch them I feel, I don't know. Too put together."

"There's nothing wrong with that."

"I wish I could exaggerate. I'd like to weigh ten pounds less, or even more, and pull it off like they do. I love their wrinkles and heavy makeup. The emphatic figures, the worn-out sandals."

"Why?"

"Because it means they're above perfection. Because they don't worry about it, which only makes them more beautiful. Because life marks their faces, and they live hard."

"And we don't?"

As they speak, on all sides of them, the piazza keeps filling with more people, more laughter, more affectionate greetings.

She withdraws her hand from his and removes a series of pins from her hair, letting it down. She says: "With one of these women, you'd have had another life, a different family."

"Of course. And so would you, with your Roman boyfriend."

A group has formed in front of the couple, several generations of a family. The grandmother is still young, a bit chubby. Her hair is dark and short, her lipstick deep red. She holds her granddaughter by the fingertips and helps her step on and off the sidewalk. She dedicates all her attention to their little game. The little girl wobbles, full of excitement and trepidation. At one point she lets go of the grandmother and manages to take a few awkward steps on her own.

The child's mother is a tall, statuesque woman. She wears a sundress and is very visibly pregnant. She's talking to other people and isn't looking at her daughter. The couple observes the scene, but neither the grandmother nor the little girl is aware of being watched. The wife opens and closes the zipper of her purse a few times.

"Do you remember that moment?" he asks.

She shifts her gaze to the little girl's mother and says: "It's years since I've worn a pretty sundress like that. I used to have so many, who knows where they ended up?"

"We were in the kitchen of our old house."

"This dress doesn't really flatter me, I don't think."

"We were cooking together."

Now she glances over at the playground.

"Wasn't it a Sunday morning? Weren't we at the park?"

"No, we were home, it was evening. When I looked up he was cutting across the length of the dining room, confident as can be, pushed forward by some mysterious force."

By now the piazza is buzzing with activity. In the distance, a band has begun to play. Every bench is taken up, every coffee bar full, and more and more people are looking out their windows.

"That's not how I recall it. In my memory, we were at the park, it was sunny."

"You're misremembering."

"Or you are."

"How could we have two completely different memories of that moment? The first time he walked on his own?"

"Let it go. Anyway, I don't think he would have come to Rome with us on this trip."

"Sure he would have, to celebrate your birthday."

"He'd have been bored, at twenty-three, hanging out with us."

"Maybe he'd have brought a girlfriend."

As they speak, still seated on the low wall, a few women, all middle-aged, gather around them. They have cropped hair and large breasts and comfortable sandals, and they're wearing short-sleeved cotton dresses. They take seats in a row along the wall, beside the wife. Only one woman remains standing, and she seems a bit put out.

The wife gets up abruptly and steps aside.

"*Prego,*" she says.

The standing woman sits down right away, without thanking her.

"Why did you give up your spot?" the husband asks.

"I don't know. Because I felt in the way."

"You're the one who wanted to come early. Sit here," he says. But as soon as he stands up, the pregnant woman takes his place. "Now we'll have to stand in the sun the entire time."

"Let's go back."

"Back where?"

"To the apartment."

"Now?"

"Yes, now."

"What about the Virgin? The music's getting louder, she must be close."

"I don't feel like waiting for her anymore."

"What do you mean? You've been talking to me about this procession for months."

The piazza, by now overflowing with people, has turned pleasantly rowdy. The procession is approaching the crowd, though the Virgin has yet to make her appearance. It's hard to notice the tears in the woman's eyes. No one, apart from the husband, who holds her in his arms, pays them heed.

· 3 ·

The couple has returned to the apartment. A breeze stirs the curtains in the living room window. He's eating a slice of pizza bianca on the couch and reading a guidebook. She's sitting at the piano and pressing on keys. She leafs through the lesson book on the piano stand.

"Where's the trattoria we're going to tonight? Can we walk there?" he asks.

"A family used to live here."

"If there's time, I'd like to walk over to the church of Santa Cecilia."

"There was a little boy or girl who took piano lessons. I see notes from whoever taught them."

"Do you know the church of Santa Cecilia?"

She doesn't reply. She walks into the dining room and opens the crockery cupboard. The hinges squeak. The insides of the cupboard doors are lined with cheery turquoise paper. She looks at all the tablecloths folded and stacked inside. She breathes in their smell.

"Let's eat at home. It's hot, some melon and prosciutto will be fine."

"What about the reservation?"

"We can go another day."

"You keep changing your mind."

She starts to clear off the surface of the dining table, gathering up the objects in batches and moving them into another room.

"What are you doing now?"

"Setting the table. I'll put this stuff on the bed for now."

"Can't we eat at the small table in the kitchen?"

"Let's eat here."

"Under the chandelier that makes you nervous?"

"Yes."

After she's cleared everything off the table she pulls out

a tablecloth and spreads it on top, then closes the cupboard doors. She makes several trips to the kitchen and returns with two plates, silverware, napkins, glasses, place mats, a jug of water. She plants two candles into the silver candlesticks. She asks:

"Why don't we have a cupboard like this, lined with pretty paper? With all the tablecloths so nicely organized, one for each day of the week?"

"You always complain that tablecloths get stained."

"We should also get those thick fragrant soaps for the bathroom, the ones that foam up. They make you want to wash your hands every time you see them."

"Don't you like our house?"

"I'm just asking."

"Asking what?"

"What it would have been like to raise our son in a place like this."

He closes the guidebook and sets it on the coffee table. Then he stands and walks over to the window, nudging the curtains apart and looking outside for a moment with his back to his wife.

"Different."

"Would he have slept in the room that's locked?"

"Stop."

"Would he have played with other kids in that piazza?"

"Don't ask these questions. Please."

"And when the ball slipped away and he ran after it, what if we were here, not there?"

He turns around to look at his wife, who is still fussing with the table.

"He was twelve years old. He knew how to cross the street."

She returns to the piano and starts rummaging again through the bowl of keys. Taking the whole bowl with her, she vanishes down the corridor. She comes back a minute later, frustrated.

"The keys don't work."

"What are you trying to open?"

"The room that's locked."

"That room's not for us."

"I just want to see it."

He pours a glass of water from the jug on the table and offers it to his wife.

"Drink this. Take a bath. In a little bit I'll make dinner and we can open a bottle of wine."

She drinks some water. In her other hand she's still holding the bowl of keys. She finishes drinking and gives the glass to her husband. She tells him:

"Let's go."

"Where?"

"Let's leave."

"What are you saying?"

"I don't want to spend the next six weeks in Rome. I want to go back to our house. And I want to leave this one in the meantime."

"We've already rented it."

"Plans change."

"It's lovely, it's comfortable, there's a nice breeze that blows through. You were just going on about the soap."

"I'd rather sleep in a hotel with other tourists. I can't stay here anymore."

Without warning she throws the bowl full of keys on the floor. All the keys scatter across the parquet, around their feet. She asks her husband, calmly and quietly: "Why won't that room open?"

He doesn't answer. On all fours, he begins to gather the scattered keys from the floor. He sets the bowl on top of the piano and says:

"Get ahold of yourself. There's nothing waiting for you in that room. Nothing but the grief already inside you."

She sits on the piano bench and looks at the lesson book. She studies the notes, absorbed by them, comprehending nothing of what they mean. She raises her hands as if she's about to play, but then she makes two fists that land lightly on the keys, producing a disagreeable sound. She draws the lid over the piano keys. When all is quiet again, she gets up and searches for her cell phone. She finds it on the table. She sits down and dials a number, waits for it to ring, then says slowly, in Italian, "*Buona sera,* do you have a double room available for tonight?"

She waits for an answer and is about to say something when she's interrupted by a deafening noise inside the house, coming from another room. The crash is violent, overwhelming.

He rushes to check the rooms, but she stays seated at the table, motionless, under the chandelier. Eventually, she ends the call and sets down her cellphone beside an empty plate.

"What happened?" she asks her husband when he returns.

"One of the French doors in the kitchen slammed shut."

"And?"

"It cracked. A section of the glass shattered."

He walks over to his wife, sits beside her at the table.

"Now what do we do?"

"We need to call someone to fix it. And let the landlords know."

"Will they be upset?"

"These things happen. It was windy."

"Who can fix this sort of thing?"

"I don't know, we'll have to ask in a hardware store. Is there glass all over the place?"

"I'm afraid so. The shards still attached to the doorframe are dangerous."

"I'll go look. There's a broom on the balcony, behind the washing machine."

"Be careful. I'd wear a pair of gloves."

She stands up. Before going to the kitchen she touches her husband's shoulder and says:

"I'm sorry we missed the procession."

"It doesn't matter."

"I wanted to take you."

"You'll always remember it."

"But you won't."

"Next year he'll have been gone as many years as he was alive."

"I know."

She switches on the chandelier. The light, strong and unpleasant, transforms the darkening space into something like a glaring operating room in which, on a Saturday afternoon eleven years before, the doctors had done all they could.

"So we'll stay?" he asks.

"Yes, I'm sorry."

"It's okay."

"You were right, we should have put a weight in front of those doors."

"Should we go to the hardware store tomorrow?"

"Tomorrow's Sunday, they'll be closed."

"Right."

"If we get up early we can go to Porta Portese. Before it gets too hot."

"What's there?"

"Pretty much everything. We'll get lost, you'll like it."

Notes

I N A CITY where water stains everything it touches, I'd notice when washing the dishes that the faucet and the sink and even the glasses I'd just rinsed and dried were mottled by a kind of hazy mildew, and this annoyed me. My husband explained that these faint stains were a form of lime scale, and that I'd have to scrub hard with vinegar, or else slice a lemon in half and run it over the surface, to restore the shine. It was a trick he'd picked up at one of his first jobs, before he started at the butcher's, working in a trattoria kitchen, where he'd learned to prepare a series of foreign dishes, to drain the pasta at just the right moment and sauté chicory greens in a pan. At the end of the evening, when the owner, who was also the chef, plunked himself down at a table with a glass of mirto to chat with a few of the regulars, it was up to my husband to clean the kitchen, which he had to leave sparkling for the owner's mother, who lived above the restaurant and who'd come down in the morning to prepare the fruit tarts in peace and quiet.

I understood this woman's stipulations even though I'd

never met her. I, too, like to keep a neat house, with everything in its place. Even as a young girl, I was perhaps a bit too zealous in helping my mother (who was somewhat disorderly and distracted) to organize jars in the kitchen, shoes and sandals kicked off by the door, notebooks and books always stacked on the beat-up iron table where my brothers and I did our homework. An empty cup abandoned on a stool or a pencil left for a moment on the windowsill was enough to irk me; I insisted on finding the perfect location for every object scattered about the rooms, otherwise I couldn't truly relax. When I closed my eyes to sleep at night, I'd picture the *alna,* a wooden rack where, amid the jumble of my brothers' clothes, my school uniform was laid out, one clean set and one backup, which I itched to rehang neatly; or else I thought of how satisfying it would be to dig my nail beneath the film of soap scum lining the soap dish here and there and scrape away the excess.

In this city with its tarnishing water I raised two remarkably messy twins. Even the hospital where I gave birth to them sprang from the water, looking almost like a giant ship forever moored in the middle of the river, which to me was the color of tea with a few spoonfuls of milk. The next thing I knew the twins were grown, gangly, shaving in the mornings and going out on their own in the evenings, who knows where, spending hours with their friends, chatting and flirting even though neither of them ever brought a girl home for me to meet. They were comfortable with their peers, they dressed and talked and laughed like everyone else even though they were different. They were fifteen when I became a widow.

It was a Sunday and I was working for a tailor shop at the other end of the city. It was open seven days a week. I was adjusting hemlines and fixing zippers, and sadly the twins were the ones to find their father in our bedroom, already dead from heart failure. They thought he was taking a long nap, but instead he'd left without saying a word to anyone.

They told me my husband had taken a shower just before lying down, so his hair was still damp. I think this is why both of the twins became EMTs. And I'm truly proud of them, always ready to rush in and help no matter the emergency. On the phone they talk about where they've been, the cities hit by earthquakes, or out on the highway where everyone drives like a maniac. Though for the most part, they say, they're in and out of private homes, where someone's suffering from acute appendicitis, or has broken a leg, or succumbs to the same sudden illness that took their father. After twenty years the twins have officially separated, in the sense that they now live in two different places, and it strikes me that they've both chosen to live in small island towns. They say they don't miss hectic city life, so they rarely come back to see me, but I understand, they're caught up with their jobs and that's a good thing.

For years now, I've been washing the dishes less often, letting them pile up for a couple of days. There's no dinner to make anymore for my husband or the twins, who usually went out and ate junk food while we were under the same roof anyway. I'll sometimes go several days using only one glass. Which means I've been able to work more hours down in the basement at the tailor's—she, too, is a widow from another continent—shortening and lengthening hems, taking in and letting out piles of skirts and pants. The commute takes me almost an hour, riding the tram across the city to nearly the end of the line, but if I'm able to find a window seat and look out I don't get bored. Which is how I always end up seeing the hospital where the twins were born, and crowds of people wandering along the tree-lined avenue or dining on wide sidewalks. The tailor's space is cramped, freezing in winter but cool in summer. My spot is at the back of the basement, which I like—there's a counter along the wall with a row of clear plastic bottles with no labels, each holding small buttons of different types and colors. Amid the chaos of other people's clothing and scraps of leftover fabric, those little bottles are a refuge of order and joy. Down there, while I work beneath the fluorescent lights, I listen to music from my country. The tailor, who has many clients, is a well-meaning but harried woman. I think she struggles to keep up with the rent, which is why she often can't pay me everything I'm owed at the end of the week. When she goes on vacation for a few days or has an appointment, I run the shop on my own, sometimes taking the clients' measurements even though they don't trust me, they prefer the tailor to do that.

The hours at the tailor's sail by, there's always something to adjust or a last-minute job, but I do get antsy sitting beneath those fluorescent tubes with their harsh, wavering light, rattling now and then, and emitting a disturbing buzz. Though at least at the tailor's I can avoid the sensation I sometimes feel at home, a pang in my chest, my breath caught for a moment in the night, a wave of sadness that rises from my stomach and clogs my throat: all tied to the equally wonderful and painful memory of having raised two sons and having once been a wife within those walls.

At the tailor's I can avoid the minor torment, in the evenings, of having to turn the lights on in every room of the apartment. I leave the door to the twins' room open, even though it pains me every time I glance at their two single beds with no headboards, the dresser between them, the shadows and wrinkles on their bedspreads. When they left home it was as if I gave birth a second time, and I say second because in my mind that first time at the hospital was only one birth. Living alone for the first time in my life seemed just as revolutionary a moment, though without that same joy, as if I'd passed into a realm of continuous worry. It's strange that maternal anxiety grows with time, that you get worse with the years. I'd have thought the opposite, but how can we bear the distances, the absences, the silences our own children generate?

One day at the tailor's I ran into a teacher from the twins' elementary school. She'd always been my favorite, the only one who understood that the other kids sometimes made fun of my boys, the only one who smiled when I came to pick them up in the afternoon and who admired my flared and colorful cotton dresses. That day she'd brought in a long gown she wanted to adjust—she'd put on a little weight—explaining that she had a wedding to attend at the end of the month. She was saddened to hear of my husband's passing, but happy to hear of the twins' jobs and their island lives. While I ran pins up her body, she told me that the school, where she still taught, was looking for someone to keep an eye on the kids for an hour or so, to give the teachers a chance to have their lunch or run errands, since the woman who normally did this had just had surgery and would need a couple of weeks to recover.

I liked the idea of going back to that school every day, the way I once did. It had been ages since I'd woken up and made breakfast in time to cram myself on the bus with the twins,

standing the entire way to that distant and sleepy neighborhood you passed on the way to the airport. No one ever gave
up their seat, and if we spoke in our own language, the elderly
passengers would stare. In any case, it's all transformed into a
pleasant memory. Those days the twins were either at school
or with me, never anywhere else; I always knew where they
were, and how.

The school is on a side street, with no stores around. It felt
as familiar as if I'd been there yesterday, so after I got off the
bus I stopped at my usual snack bar to have a juice, served to
me by the same bald barista with the red apron, who even
gave me a subtle nod of recognition. I was astonished that he
was still there, the same man, after all that time, and just as
astonished at myself, too, for having lived so long in the same
city, and for having spent twenty years on the other side of
the world. Then I made the long trek to the school, down a
road flanked by five- or six-story buildings and cars parked on
either side. I didn't know anyone who lived in the area and
yet I still felt I belonged there in some way, perhaps because
of all the memories, and as I walked I could still feel the presence of the twins holding my hands, the two of them talking
in their high-pitched voices, clinging to me all the way there
until they flitted off and disappeared inside the school.

I checked in at the administration desk and a woman
explained the job. That day all I had to do was fill out a stack
of forms. The woman showed me where the nurse's office
was, in case one of the kids got hurt, and then she brought
me outside so I could see where they played. After that she
walked me down a hallway where there was a restroom and
a place for me to store my things, including my purse, so that

I'd have nothing to distract me from the children. It was a kind of storage closet, with a door that didn't lock, though in any case there was a custodian who stood guard at the school entrance. I'd have to skip lunch, which I told her was fine, I'd have a hearty breakfast. I could no longer picture the twins at that age, now that their voices had changed and they towered over me. And yet they'd once squealed like the children all around.

My first day on the job I was nervous, so much so that at the snack bar on the way to the school I was tempted to resort to a strange and secret habit that had comforted me as a little girl: to chew, every evening, on a piece of napkin, which I'd grab in the mornings for just that purpose from the bakery on the ground floor of our building. After dinner I'd secretly tear off a piece, keep it in my mouth, and then throw it away. What I liked most was how it dissolved on my tongue, though never completely, and how its bland but comforting flavor would gradually seep from the napkin's fibers into my body. It was a source of immense pleasure and never once did me harm, a superstitious ritual that inexplicably calmed me down. I did it to ward off all forms of bad luck, to make sure my mother didn't get sick, for example, or to keep from having nightmares. At one point or another I stopped. Who knows, maybe I should have kept on with it, maybe then my husband wouldn't have died on our bed that afternoon with his hair damp and not a word of warning. So I grabbed a napkin and put it in my raincoat pocket for good luck, that's all.

It had been an unusual spring, filled with rain and biting winds, but now finally the weather had turned. Only the mornings were chilly, and like everyone else I kept my rain-coat on. But by afternoon, you'd be dying of heat and would have to take it off. So I'd hang my raincoat in the storage closet, set my zipped-up purse on a stool, and head out to take my post. Every now and then I had to escort a child to the bathroom or retrieve a ball thrown over the gate. But no major emergencies or injuries, not even a bee like the one that once stung one of the twins while he was watching TV with his hand stuffed between the couch cushions—poor thing, the hand swelled right up and for a few weeks he had to keep out of the sun and wear a glove made of gauze. Some of the kids chose not to play, they'd sit in a row and watch the others as if they were already bored adults. There were a few choking scares, when water went down the wrong pipe, or when a kid put something he shouldn't in his mouth, a bottle cap or a pen cap, which meant there was no time to run to the nurse and I'd have to stick a finger down a throat to find the object, holding his jaw open to help him spit it out, just as I'd done with the twins in years past. I was so happy to spend a little time outside and feel the heat on my skin, something I missed down in the tailor's basement beneath the fluorescent lights.

After a few days I settled into a rhythm, eating a second breakfast before heading to the school and having a bite afterward at the same snack bar, where you could get a hot meal at lunch. The man who helped the chef there was from my country, and when he saw me come in he'd put some spice into the dishes. I was always starving. I never thought that being on my feet for an hour would be so tiring, but it was. One day, after eating a plate of rice and vegetables, I was digging around in my raincoat pocket to pay the cashier when I fished out a small slip of paper, folded up a few times. I thought it was something I'd left there, a receipt or a tram ticket I'd absentmindedly crumpled on the ride over, or maybe that lucky napkin I'd grabbed and forgotten about the following day. But no, it was a long strip of paper someone had torn off by hand, with a few words written on it: "We don't like you."

The handwriting, in pencil, was childlike, as if the author were still learning to write, the letters all askew. I felt a pang of insult, but it didn't fully sink in; it was like the slip of a dull knife while you're idly chopping onions, causing a vaguely irksome cut but not a bloody one. I was convinced that I wasn't the intended recipient, that it was addressed to someone else, something meant for one of the children, which for whatever reason had ended up in my raincoat pocket in the confusion of the school day. Truly that's what I thought, and I didn't think about it again. But then a few days later, at the end of my shift, when I reached into that same raincoat pocket, a similar slip of paper was waiting for me.

This time there was a different message: "We don't like your face." Again the handwriting looked childlike, again the words were in pencil. I was still at school, in that narrow hallway, and this time I felt a wave of sickness, like a light punch to the stomach, and I thought I might cry. Still, I didn't say anything to anyone. I didn't even know where to turn. Almost nobody at the school said hello to me. The teacher who'd suggested the job was out on a field trip, and the others all ignored me. Only a few of the children cast me a smile on occasion. Three more days went by. The third note contained just two words: "You're dirty." This made me feel truly awful. I thought of my immaculate home and the trattoria kitchen my husband left sparkling. The next day I decided not to wear my raincoat even though it was drizzling that morning, just to see what would happen. That afternoon I found a note stuffed in my purse. This time it read, "We don't want you to stay here." I was shaken. Someone had obviously opened my purse. Everything was still there: my keys, my wallet and the money inside it, my lipstick, my glasses. They hadn't stolen a cent.

That day, too, I didn't mention the notes to anyone. I decided to keep my purse on me, slung over my shoulder, but the women in the administration office noticed immediately and told me I couldn't work without my body and hands completely free, even though I spent nearly the entire time there standing and watching the children run and jump around.

At first I'd liked going to the school in the mornings, but now I was fearful, constantly on edge, to the point where I couldn't wait for the job to end. Around that time one of the twins called, and when I told him about what had happened he was furious. He told me I needed to speak with the principal, that I could even press charges. I'll go back to that piece-of-shit school and have a few words with them, he said. But neither he nor his brother came to confront anyone. The next day I went to the teacher who'd offered me the job and showed her the four notes, which I'd been keeping in an envelope. She was a little perplexed, maybe a little embarrassed, but she tried to reassure me.

"It must be some game the kids are playing," she said.

"Then why do they end up in my pocket?" I asked. This she couldn't explain.

"Throw them away, let it go," she told me. "You're only here a short while, what's it to you?"

That was the end of it, and the job. My last day, the administrator paid me and bid me a polite goodbye. The employee I'd been subbing for had recovered from surgery and would be back the next day.

What to do with those four notes? I still had the envelope, as if it were a letter I was planning to mail, but to whom? I didn't want anyone to open it and discover what was inside. Both the twins—by now the other had called—encouraged me to save everything. In the end there were four paper slips in the envelope, all filled with creases, each with the same sort of message. But I had no desire to file any kind of report. And in every drawer, on every shelf in the house, tucked between the pages of a book, beneath a couch cushion, even in the overhead cupboard where I stored off-season clothes, the strident presence of that envelope tormented me.

I took on more hours at the tailor's, where at least I was far from the notes and felt some relief. But then something upsetting happened there, too, while the tailor had gone out for a coffee and I was alone: I got up for a second to look through the little bottles on the shelf for the right button, when a thin fluorescent lightbulb, normally mounted above my sewing machine, usually lit but for some reason switched off at that moment, detached from the ceiling and shattered with a startling crash, covering the spot where I worked with sharp, terrifying shards and scattering white powder over the fabrics, the floor, my seat. If I hadn't stepped away just then, it would have landed right on me.

Feeling quite unnerved, I called both twins and managed to get one on the phone. He was immediately alarmed, and warned me that the white substance contained mercury. Once the bulb broke, he said, it became a vapor that could spread through the room. He told me I'd need to very carefully remove every trace of it, instructing me to wear gloves and cover my mouth with a scarf, if I had one, and to otherwise touch nothing, to pick up the shards by hand without sweeping the area and to open the windows, though there was no window to speak of down in the basement and the shop door on the floor above was too far from my work space to help with circulation, which made me scared that I wouldn't be able to rid the air of the poisonous fumes. A minute later the other twin called, and he, too, was very worried.

"Tell the tailor to check the electrical system, things like that can cause a fire. And I mean it, Mamma, cover your mouth," he told me before hanging up.

I did what I could, though constantly terrified that I was getting it wrong. The more I wiped the floor with a wet cloth the more tiny glass fragments I encountered, and my scarf kept slipping from my mouth. The powder was almost blindingly white.

When the tailor came back from her coffee break, I'd already tied up the trash bag and I was exhausted.

"Was the light on?" she asked.

"It was off."

"Did you hurt yourself?"

"I don't think so. But can you call an electrician, please?"

"Move over to the other end for now," she said. "Those lights work fine."

I went back home, out of sorts, and the next day I called the tailor and told her I had a bad headache. What I really had was a giant knot in my throat along with a slightly bitter

taste, which was linked, I assumed, to the poisonous fumes. I
thought I'd stay home and organize things around the house a
little to calm myself down. But the fear of that mysteriously
exploded bulb kept coming back, and, behind that unease, the
equally inexplicable story of the paper slips. All of a sudden
it felt hot and I was sweating. I lost the mood to clean—I had
no desire to organize my sock drawer, throw away expired
creams, or find a new way to store my pots and pans. After my
efforts from the day before, I was drained.

I sat down at the table in front of a whirling box fan. And
there I opened the envelope and removed the notes—I'd hidden it in a biscuit tin, stuffed in the storage shed on the terrace,
between the brooms. Since they were all written in pencil, I
did my best to erase the words, leaving only a pale remnant.
Then I began tearing them with my fingers into little pieces.
At first I worked slowly, though with increasing pleasure,
enjoying the challenge. As someone who can thread even the
tiniest of needles, I consider myself quite dexterous. Soon I'd
built a small white mound on the table before me. The bits of
paper looked almost like the thick grains of sugar you'd sprin-
kle on top of a panettone or a colomba or certain cookies, the
kind I would sometimes buy to decorate the twins' birthday
cake. They shifted a little in the wind from the fan, some trembling, some even lifting off. I thought of gathering them all
in a water bottle like the tailor's buttons. But then one of the
bits leaped up and landed straight in my mouth, like an insect
flitting about the park in the evening. And before I could spit
it out it dissolved on my tongue, as if it really were a grain of
sugar.

I knew right away what I needed to do, and began feeding the bits of paper into my mouth one by one. They dissolved in an instant, leaving behind a not unpleasant taste on my tongue. It didn't take me long, no more than ten minutes, and soon enough those messages disappeared along with the bitter taste in my throat.

Dante Alighieri

· 1 ·

A T SEVENTEEN I'd kissed no one. But my best friend
since childhood had: after years of dramatic, dead-end
crushes, whose ups and downs we'd analyze in exacting detail,
she started dating S, a spry, sarcastic boy two years older than
we were, who was already a student at the university in the
small wooded town where I was born and raised, with humid
summers and snowy winters, not far from the raging Atlantic Ocean. When S went to our high school he ignored us. In
those days, he was madly in love with an older girl, and the
two of them seemed to have been dating since forever, locked
in a precociously serious relationship. But then he broke up
with her, and one day at summer's end S and my friend met by
chance on the seafront, and talked for a bit, and a few days later
he called her up and asked her to the movies.

My friend, in turns insecure and intrepid, loved the stage.
And what had happened was that S came back to our high
school one evening to see a play at the end of the school year,

because his younger brother was in the orchestra, and my friend had a big role in that play. It was there, while she was in costume and heavily made up, pretending to be a tormented thirty-year-old, that he fell for her. Naturally my friend described every last thing about the hours she spent with S—he studied literature and was mad about Charlie Chaplin—with exuberance and enthusiasm, usually in the evenings over the telephone when we should have been doing our homework. And so she told me about their first kiss: after the second time they went to the movies, at night, they went back to the beach, where they'd first run into each other, to talk and walk. They'd climbed up into a lifeguard's chair that had yet to be removed for the colder months, squeezing together in that austere wooden throne where someone typically keeps an eye out for signs of danger and distress. That was where my friend felt S's lips on hers, and the unexpected impact of his face rubbing her skin here and there like sandpaper. At the same time, she felt his fingers on her back and heard the crashing of the waves in the background while their hair blew about every which way.

I absorbed these private revelations with a tremor impossible to ignore. On the one hand, I felt excluded, left behind, but at the same time I knew how much it mattered to my friend to confess all this to me and to no one else. She would go out with S for two hours, then call me, and we'd talk about it for four, which was why I was able to imagine what went on between them and to feel even more connected to her. I believed I had an important role, and in some way participated (invisibly, of course) in their relationship. It was just that she was the one in the throes of it, the one with a boyfriend, the one who'd crossed an emotional threshold—namely, the anxiety of never coupling up that looms over at least a part of everyone's adolescence—while I, her faithful audience, waited my turn.

Unfortunately—even if it's wrong to start things off with that adverb—about a year later, at my friend's birthday party, in a Chinese restaurant with a few other friends, S, who was by then her steady boyfriend, realized he was undeniably in love with me. That night, given that he barely looked at me, I suspected nothing; he seemed as devoted as ever to my friend, with his long arm resting over her chair and his hand mussing up her cropped hair now and then. But a few days later—it was a Saturday—my father, who had gone out to fetch the newspaper, discovered a letter with no stamp in our mailbox under the low-spreading red maple tree. The envelope, addressed in blue ballpoint, was intended for me, and in the top corner, in place of the sender's name, it said DANTE ALIGHIERI in capital letters. My father, who taught economics at the university, who came from the other side of the world, and had no idea who the real Dante Alighieri was, handed me the envelope without comment.

I rushed to my room, perched on the edge of my bed, and studied the penmanship before opening the envelope. There were a few handwritten pages inside. I no longer remember exactly what the letter said. There was a puzzling reference to a popular song during which, according to S, you could hear my name in the background over and over again. He'd been listening to the song for weeks in order to feel closer to me. I can still recall the impact of those pages, all those words, surely more intense and upsetting than the sensation I'd struggled to envision of his rough skin against my face. The handwriting itself felt like a dense cage around the heart of that poor boy. It was a letter filled with affliction and adoration mixed up with feelings of guilt. He'd been thinking about me secretly for months, he confessed. Whenever we ran into each other, at one of my friend's plays, or if I happened to be hanging out with her when they met up at the movies or wherever. On those occasions I would wait until they kissed to reestablish contact before saying my goodbyes and handing her off to him. But in his letter S claimed that he no longer loved my friend, that when he kissed her he thought of me, that he'd slept poorly for weeks and had nearly stopped eating. He dreamed of me all night and he suffered, during the day, from visions in which every girl on the street turned into a version of me. Once, as he dreamed of me at the beach, I had even miraculously materialized. At the end of the letter he said he'd written a second letter to my friend to say that their relationship was over. He added: "I know you love me, too."

I was struck, first off, by the method of delivery: I knew S didn't drive, that he had yet to get his license (something my friend would complain about), and the fact that he'd arrived at my family's home on foot, likely in the dark, maybe holding a flashlight, in a town where everyone drove everywhere, rendered him unique, romantic, even heroic from my point of view. He must have walked who knows how many hours to deposit that envelope, his heart beating fast as I slept, I thought to myself. Had he lingered a few minutes under the windows of our house trying to guess which was mine? Had he delivered his harsh letter to my friend before or after he'd delivered the one to me?

Feeling desired for the first time in my life, I was discombobulated. And I was also—I can't deny it—flattered. I couldn't believe I'd caused the suffering and dreams and sleepless nights of another person. But the really astonishing thing was the way he ended the letter: *I know you love me, too.* As soon as I read that line I realized he was right, that I was just as in love with S as my friend was, and that I'd been waiting for him to love me in return. It was that impudent sentence, along with the outrageous pseudonym he'd chosen, that won me over and made me feel like a worm at the same time.

I don't remember the exact events—phone calls? more letters?—that ended up bringing us together one Saturday morning on a bench in the middle of a deserted campus. It was July and the air was still and stifling, buildings empty, books returned to the library. In other words, it was that total calm and desolation that mark the end of every semester. I felt confused and awkward, and the first thing I said was that I didn't want to cause my friend further pain. After I'd replaced her, she'd sunk into worrisome depression. I'd gone to see her and say I was sorry, to talk things over, in the bedroom where we'd spent so many happy hours together, but her parents had looked at me askance. My friend was collapsed on the bed, her shoulders turned away from me, and she was crying. I said hi and she muttered something back. I saw her face was pale, her hair greasy. She hadn't left the house or bathed for days, and I remember I was distracted by a sour smell in the air. "I thought you were my best friend," she said, thereby letting me know that I no longer was. "You've ruined everything."

S, when we met, was also pale and distraught. He'd been reading a book while waiting for me on the bench, bent over himself, and when I sat down beside him he couldn't look me in the face, either. He didn't seem happy to see me. In fact, having me there beside him, and (if he desired) all to himself, seemed to torment him all the more. Of the three of us I was the only one who sat up straight, more or less lucid in spite of my jumbled feelings. In that sense the two of them were still together, while I remained the outsider, even though I'd been cast into the center of the tragedy. I wavered for a long while on that bench, but in the end, in front of those sad and empty buildings, I turned S down in order to salvage (so I thought) what I considered at the time to be an important long-term friendship. And he, with great dignity but also great disappointment, accepted my reasoning, adding that my sacrifice was an act of considerable grace and tremendous loyalty, which only made him admire me all the more.

He opened his book to cite something he'd underlined: "Every desire becomes a decision." It was from the diary of a famous author, he explained, and then he said: "You'll do something amazing with your life," as if he were an oracle, and after that he asked me to tell him something about my childhood. All told, it was a reasonable request, even though deep down I was thinking, or maybe hoping, that he'd have asked me for a kiss, just one lacerating kiss, which I'd already granted him in my head. I waited for him to stealthily draw close, to place a hand on my knee, for our eyes to close before feeling the impact of his lips and the smell of his mouth. I craved a reckless move, one that would turn my schoolgirl sacrifice on its head. Instead he listened, all the while maintaining a respectable distance between us. So I told him about one of the things I did for fun when I was little, when I'd go into the woods behind our house where a brook flowed, searching for life under the rocks. I'd turn the rocks over—some of them were heavy—exposing worms and insects that trembled and twisted in the sunlight. I'd look at these life-forms with horror and fascination, without ever disturbing them. They were obscure, armored organisms, and some looked prehistoric. I would study them, but only for so long, then I'd replace the heavy lid and leave them there in peace, in their hidden, restless cosmos. S didn't react, he didn't ask me anything else, he just listened. I didn't tell him that, for much of my life, I felt in league with those invisible creatures, and that with his love letter he'd been the one to lift the rock. Of course I now realize that our relationship, or at least the possibility of a relationship, was the equivalent of that minuscule but frenzied display of life, exposed for a moment, only a moment, before the lid came back down.

· 2 ·

But what does this preamble have to do with today? Why are these repressed, still muddled recollections teeming in my head as I'm seated on a church pew at the funeral of a woman who was once my mother-in-law? *Mostraci come vivere ogni ora che fugge come la tua ora, come l'ultima ora, e come offrirtela con tutta la nostra anima.*

For years, nearly every Sunday, I used to have lunch with the woman lying in the coffin: first when she was the one to open the door for us and prepare a three-course meal, then when we were the ones to bring food, and in the end when her caretaker heated up some soup for everyone, which she would barely sip, munching instead on a few apple slices. The caretaker is here today, along with my husband; his rumpled hair is white now, his black jacket pinches slightly at the shoulders, and his face, still handsome, is tense with grief. A man with whom I lived rather happily for twenty-five years. In front of the basilica, a short while ago, we hugged and kissed one another. But he entered with a willowy woman, with a stiff back and long dark, curly hair. They're sitting side by side. I recognize her: she lives in that Fascist-era building close to ours, on the other side of the steps, and she's always out walking a gray dog that's thin like her. In front of the basilica, my husband told me that my mother-in-law had just been dressed by her nurse after her morning sponge bath when her heart stopped, with no one near and dear at her side. Our daughter, my mother-in-law's only grandchild, isn't even here to attend the funeral. Right after high school she moved up north. It's been a while since we've spoken, and at the moment she's out on a ship, to help people who risk their lives in flimsy boats on the open sea, trying to get to Italy.

I, too, just got here, this morning, after crossing the Atlantic comfortably by plane. For seven years, ever since my husband and I decided to separate, I've lived between two continents; it's feasible, or at least that's what I tell myself, even though the preposition makes it sound like eternal limbo. At the end of August I leave my Roman life behind, I say goodbye to the Mediterranean, and return to that raging ocean I know so well. In May I head back to Italy. But I'm here now, too, at the end of October, because I have a week off, and I'll come again for a month at Christmas. When I landed this morning, at dawn, the airport was empty and I got straight into a taxi. It's a trip I make so often that I don't even look up as the taxi driver speeds along the freeway between Fiumicino and Rome. What strikes me instead, as the plane lands, is the bird's-eye view from high up where Lazio's thin white coast meets the sea, a strip of land that, in its sands, in the beach bars, and in the waves, contains a portion of my life—as mother and wife—that's come to an end. Only from that vantage point am I able to realize just how narrow a space we're allotted, compared to the infinite expanse of the water, for all our gripes and days on earth.

In the taxi I checked my text messages, and that's how I learned, not from my husband but from a chat organized by a mutual friend, that my mother-in-law, who'd recently been moved to a nursing home, had died the day before, and that the funeral would take place this afternoon.

I paid the taxi driver, I crossed the crowded street with my suitcase, and I greeted the doorman, who welcomed me back and handed me the pile of bills that had accrued. I rode up in the elevator, I turned the key three times to the left to open the door, but almost immediately I went out again, to have a coffee at the bar beneath my building, to enjoy the lingering autumn sunshine, to say hi to a few neighbors, to buy milk and bread and make an appointment at the hair salon. I quickly circled the piazza to rouse the part of me that lives here, that still lives part-time in Rome. Every time I come back I feel rejuvenated—and also like a kind of ghost, picking up its former life in fits and starts. I went back upstairs to open the windows and let in some fresh air, to water the plants and pull out bath towels. There's always need for a small exorcism, given that when I don't live in this apartment I rent it out for short intervals, sometimes longer ones, to people I've never met, who come on vacation from all over the world and leave behind the tacit residue of their happiness.

I chose a black dress from the wardrobe I keep locked when

I'm away. I opened a drawer, which I also keep locked, and chose a pair of earrings my mother-in-law gave me after my daughter was born. I wanted to make a more thorough grocery list, so I pulled my favorite fountain pen out of the same drawer, a pen I've been using since I was twenty-one years old. My parents gave it to me when I graduated from college, even though I'd picked it out on my own (my parents were always at a loss for what to give me as a gift, always asking for specific suggestions, and eventually just started giving money to spend as I pleased). Today, unfortunately, as soon as I took the pen in hand, it slipped: the tip of the nib struck the marble floor, disrupting the flow of ink, which is why every sentence I'll write from now on will be accompanied by the stutter of a broken line, and an annoying scraping sound.

At the hair salon, where I was already dressed for the funeral, I relaxed under the heat lamp as the color soaked into my graying roots. I flipped through a few newspapers, meanwhile keeping an eye on the medieval basilica where the coffin had already arrived. It upset me to witness this somber scene invaded by tourists, lovers, waiters trying to lure passersby into their drab and overpriced restaurants.

Now it's three-thirty, and a yellow light slants in through the basilica windows. It strikes four different points along the architrave on one side of the nave. I doubt that the curly-haired neighbor sitting next to my husband even knew my mother-in-law. Or did she? Do she and my husband go walking their dogs together, in the morning? Surely they met up in the park where my husband likes to go running; one day, the conversation must have gone on. I glance up and follow the light crossing the nave. The wooden ceiling of the church looks like an orderly labyrinth of stars and octagons: a multicolored slab full of cavities. Above the altar there's a divine figure attached to the ceiling, gazing down. Her hands are raised, her palms facing toward us. It's meant to be a benediction, but it also seems as if she's warding us off. And if I, too, were to survey my life from above? Would I gain some perspective? Or would it only upset me? *I loro occhi si sono chiusi su ciò che ci seduce, su ciò che ci fa smarrire.*

· 3 ·

My parents were totally oblivious to my first romantic crisis. They tended to be unaware of my thoughts, problems, and worries. They didn't ask many questions, as if their curiosity, once activated, would reveal too much about the creature they'd made together. They accepted that we had different tastes; at the supermarket, there were items in the cart designated for me alone, for the sandwiches I took to school and for my snacks. They preferred to keep an eye on me from a distance, always cautiously, which made me feel like a dark, armored organism in their eyes. At dinner, conversation was scant; at home, we played hosts to silence, as if it were a relative who lived discreetly among us, who came out of his room for meals, who joined us only when we were together and toward whom we had to behave with attention and respect.

That silence ate a portion of every meal at the table, it breathed the air in the dining room and settled into an armchair after dinner on the nights we all sat in the living room to watch the evening news. It was with us in the car the day my parents drove me to college—not far from where we lived, about an hour away, a cozy all-girls school, where my mother, a foreigner, who'd studied at home before marrying my father, had insisted on putting the sheets on my new bed. She'd cried, a lot, when she had to say goodbye, as if I were about to fly to the other side of the world alone and unwilling, as she once had. She didn't trust that bucolic atmosphere. My father, on the other hand, told me to study economics and get good grades.

To tell the truth, I, too, cried at first, in that new world— bucolic, yes, but also alienating. I didn't know anyone and even missed the familiar silence I shared with my parents; in the first few months I also realized, once and for all, that I'd lost both my best friend, who no longer spoke to me, and any chance of getting together with S, whom I dreamed of and desired even more after turning him down. I'd saved his letter and I still read it in my new room at college before falling asleep. I kept it hidden under my mattress and I would put it under my pillow before going to bed. And through that ongoing, furtive contact with his words, I really did betray my friend. I knew I had been disingenuous with S and with myself: in spite of everything, I still harbored some hope in my head.

Before leaving for college, I'd caught sight of him once more on the beach—pale as ever, worn out, rail thin. I was walking with another friend and when he saw me he looked away, as if there were too much life in me, or maybe as if I were already dead. Holed up in my little dorm room, anguished, I'd written a long love letter to S, only to throw it away. He'd have moved on to someone else, I told myself; maybe he already hears another girl's name in that same song. Surely that daring, unseasoned Dante no longer thinks about me, but I think about him: now and then he comes to mind and I wonder what became of him, given that life has landed me not far from the birthplace and tomb of the real poet.

I'll explain: instead of a real relationship with a feigned Dante, I began to study the works of the writer himself, first in translation and then in the original language. I dove headfirst, in other words, into the history and rhyme scheme and philosophy and theology and tumultuous politics of the thirteenth century. That entire medieval world, which was brand-new for me, was what I truly fell in love with: I studied until late at the library, I took pages of notes during lessons, I memorized tercets by heart. That's how I learned the real meaning of that fictitious name on the envelope, and realized that I would have been loved only in theory—that Dante Alighieri would have adored me only in his mind, that he would never have kissed me on the bench, needless to say, given that I wasn't even a girl in flesh and blood. I discovered that Dante's lines were filled with prophecies, but that those who uttered them—Tiresias, for instance, and his daughter, poor Manto, with her face turned tragically backwards—were among the damned who suffered punishments in hell.

As I made progress I decided to devote myself to the poet officially and to write, in my final year of college, a long essay on the representation of a few female characters in the *Commedia*—not exalted Beatrice or even Francesca or Pia de' Tolomei or Matilda. Rather, I was drawn to deformed, hideous women, to the Harpies and the Furies, and to Arachne, *O folle Aragne,* who challenged Minerva. My father was upset that I hadn't followed his advice and example, and when I would go home for a weekend or for the holidays he spoke to me less and less. "You're throwing away your future," he told me one day. And my mother, who never dared stand up to her husband, didn't come to my defense. They would still buy me the foods I liked that they didn't eat, to welcome me home: the grapefruits I sliced in two every morning, salt and vinegar potato chips, coffee ice cream. I'd get upset if I mixed up the ends of the grapefruit and cut it from top to bottom instead of along the equator, exposing the two longitudinal hemispheres instead of the wedges, the spine instead of the navel. In any case, the two of them no longer guided me, they hadn't for a while, just like Virgil who vanishes at a certain point in *Purgatorio,* turning us into orphans, *scemi di sé.* A bit like Nimrod, I suppose, I'd always had a language of my own that they'd never understood. The modest prize I won for my thesis puzzled them all the more, so after I graduated I took the pen they gave me, a small notebook to jot down my impressions, and with the money I'd set aside working at the library, combined with the money from the prize, I went with a few friends to visit Dante's world, which I knew only from books, with a plan to travel around for a few months before pressing on with my medieval studies.

We made our first pilgrimage to Florence, tawny and sober, then to Ravenna, blue and flat, and we ended up in Rome. One day at the bus stop in Largo Argentina I met a man. He was attractive, with emphatic eyebrows and hair long enough to cover the tops of his ears. My friends and I had been struggling to decipher the various stops listed on the signs, and he'd stepped in to help us. Then he'd sat next to me and took us to a place, unknown to tourists, we'd have never gone to otherwise. In three seconds he'd organized a dinner to introduce us to some of his friends.

He was from Rome and had never lived anywhere else. He was a doctor and specialized in kidneys, had a dog and a kind voice and many patients, and was almost twenty years older than me. He was my first boyfriend. He took me places on his motorino, to the sea and up the Appia Antica, where we kissed among the ruins. He'd never been to America and wanted to know all about it. He was amazed when I recited certain sections of the *Commedia* from memory, and when I told him I'd never had a boyfriend before. And he found certain sad stories of mine amusing, for example, that at our house there were three televisions, one for each member of the family, or that my parents physically resembled each other so much— they both had thin lips and sleepy eyes and the same wide gap between nose and mouth—that I was afraid of being the child of cousins, even though it wasn't true. One day, when we were out on a walk, my foot started to bother me, so I stopped at a cobbler to fix my shoe—a pretty, leopard-print flat with a small hole in the sole. It was a chilly little shop with dirty walls and lots and lots of shoes arranged in cubbies along a shelf. The cobbler took my shoe in his hand and studied it for a moment. Then he gave me a hard stare with his round, light-colored eyes and said: "You need to toss these out."

Every desire becomes a decision. At twenty-two, I didn't just toss out the shoe condemned by that cobbler. Bit by bit I tossed out quite a few more things. For starters, I never went back to America with my friends. Instead I made do in Rome, where I was happy. I went on to rid myself of the guilt I felt for not having studied economics, and for not having paid attention to my mother when she tried a few times to arrange a marriage for me, with the idea (I'm guessing) of linking me up with her own destiny and passing down her unhappiness.

I wasn't sorry to put a little distance between me and those two, who didn't even know what to get me for a present. I enrolled at the same university where my boyfriend had studied for so many years to become a doctor, I translated articles so that I could rent a room, and I carried on, vaguely, with my medieval studies. But it's hard to study in a new language, I struggled to follow my professors, and to be honest I preferred spending my evenings going out with my boyfriend to staying inside with books and notebooks. I preferred waking up in the mornings in his bed and seeing the breakfast tray he'd already prepared on the table, with dry toasts and jam and his beloved beat-up coffeepot. I bought clothes at sidewalk stalls and felt new fabrics and sizes and styles on my body. On Tuesdays, when he didn't have to work, we went to Ostia to eat pasta with clams and walk, first riding out on the metro but then in the Fiat Seicento he bought. And it was there, one evening, when our shadows were long on the sand, that he asked me to marry him.

I said yes, and to stay with him forever I filled out countless forms, I got a *codice fiscale,* I chose a doctor from the public health system, I got used to hanging the wash on folding racks that overtook the rooms, and to the fragrance of just-washed clothes and the marble floors inside the apartment and all the things that, slipping from my hands for no apparent reason, shattered loudly when they hit the floor. I learned how to drive a stick shift and I got a new license, memorizing the meanings of an infinite number of road signs. I bought what I didn't have, what I needed; I still remember the kind older woman with woolen trousers and a soft taupe sweater who sold me a hair dryer (she'd pulled it out of the box, then she'd turned it on for a few seconds to show me how it worked), in a tiny store that also sold knives and plates and small appliances. As I set up my new life, eagerly, I went on throwing things away: even items of clothing I'd just bought, for instance, because after a few days I was convinced they didn't flatter me, because I wanted another style, or another color, so I gave them away to my new friends or tossed them into those big yellow bins to rid my mind of them. But more than anything I was sorry to throw things out, because love had rendered me clumsy and careless, which was why I tended to ruin brand-new things, like a pair of suede boots that got stained, I have no clue how, during a big outdoor party—I thought the stains were from drops of water that would have evaporated, but no, even getting the boots dyed at the cobbler didn't help. The same destiny awaited many dresses, many blouses—I'd put them on for a dinner out, I'd get back home and discover a patch of oil or wine I couldn't remove. I would kill beautiful plants as I lifted them brusquely from their pots. When a new mattress was delivered after we got married, sheathed in plastic, I instantly made a hole in it with a pair of scissors I was using to cut the covering away, what a pity. And I wondered, as I slept on that tiny hole on the underside of the mattress, or looked at a decapitated plant, if there were a *contrapasso,* an inverse suffering to punish people who ruin things by mistake, who insist on making new lives for themselves.

"One day you'll toss me out, too, for a younger man. It's not right that I'm the only one who's loved you," my husband would joke. I'd get upset when he'd say this, I feared it was another prophecy, and I reassured him that nothing like that would ever happen. To myself I thought, foolishly, that it wasn't true, that a boy who called himself Dante Alighieri had already loved me, and this enabled me to place a nice heavy lid over that prophecy. This meant I would always stay married to my husband, that we would grow old together. He was the only man I loved, and for him I grew accustomed to the damp morning cold in winter that gave way around two o'clock, when everyone would sit outside and sunbathe. For him I learned to spend hours at the beach every summer weekend, to wear bikinis and withstand the stones and rocks underfoot before diving in, to spend long afternoons on boats where I would melt from the heat or shudder with cold, to mistrust air conditioners likely to freeze your neck or throw out your back.

I gave birth to a daughter, a clingy little girl who would follow me into the bathroom. On Sundays we would go to Ostia to have pasta with clams and to let the dog and our daughter run around, or we would visit my in-laws, the same house where my husband had been a boy and a teenager. Their house was always cold but welcoming. I had learned by then to dress differently, to wear layers. I enjoyed being in the place that contained my husband's past, his shades. I enjoyed the conversations at the table, predictable for him, illuminating to me.

I appreciated all the food my mother-in-law would make in her tiny kitchen. It was her sanctuary, with no dishwasher but a washing machine under the marble counter, next to the sink. She was the one who told me how to make the various dishes, the meatballs and the fried vegetables, who taught me to offer clementines in winter, and panettone, and walnuts to crack at the table, to bring out the coffee in small cups on a tray, then the amaro made by my father-in-law when he went to the mountains to pick gentians. My in-laws were sweet people, they were cultured, they pardoned the grave errors I would make when I spoke quickly in Italian. They would say (though it wasn't true) that I had studied Dante better than they had, but then they would practically recite entire cantos from memory with their eyes closed. We would drive home feeling extremely full, and in the car I'd marvel at the sky with that drop of pink in it to indicate the rapid arrival of evening. After those two-course Sunday feasts we would skip dinner—an herbal tea was enough, maybe a piece of fruit before going to bed, I with a combination of lightness and satisfaction I'd never felt before and have never felt since, even though, at my in-laws' table, enveloped in that tranquil sense of delight, I was quietly so thrilled that I feared I was on the edge between life and death. All this seemed to me the clearest and most convincing proof that I had made the right choice, that I'd been wise not to put the lid on this unexpected future, to have finally exposed my life to sunlight and to have reached some sort of paradise.

Once a year I traveled with my new family to visit my parents on the other side of the ocean. They lived in the same house, constructed of wood and plastic, where Dante Alighieri had delivered his letter, and they lived there with the same silence and unhappiness. My mother prepared the double bed in the guest room and my father watched his TV shows. I found loads of grapefruits to slice open in the mornings. My parents believed that living in another country for the sake of marriage was a sacrifice I'd been fated to endure as opposed to a liberation. I'd stopped studying Dante, I'd become a housewife abroad like my mother, but this coincidence didn't bring us any closer. They weren't impressed that I had grown skilled at living in a new world, that I had gained fluency in a new language (for instance, I no longer messed up the difference between a *scrocchio* and a *scricciolo,* a *diletto* and a *delitto,* a *tracolla* and a *tracollo*). Instead they talked to my husband about aches and pains that bothered them, or they asked about unemployment rates in Italy or how taxes worked. They always gave my daughter a dress that was a few sizes too big (they were always focused on the future, only rarely on the present), and soft dolls that smelled of vanilla.

They'd say, each time, that this was the year they'd come visit us. But then for some reason or another the trip wouldn't take place, and neither they nor I were terribly sorry about it. Around my parents I felt out of place, as usual: the only child of two people who had never really taken stock of the person I was. I feared I'd betrayed them just as I'd feared long ago I'd betrayed my best friend; every time I went back to that town I thought of the day I sat on the edge of her bed, feeling doomed already in that room with its sour smell, and the way her parents had looked at me askance, and how she'd declared: *You've ruined everything.*

I took my new family to walk in the woods behind the house, among leafless trees, through a landscape that was stark and gray. It looked different; they'd paved the old path along the brook with asphalt and placed benches here and there. The ground was covered with heaps of faded orange leaves. Our daughter ran ahead of us along the path, her pigtails quivering, while my husband and I noticed how the trees, when reflected in the brook, appeared upside down, so that the tops, nude in that season, seemed like roots that extended endlessly into the black water. They were like my life: turned on its head. At the age of thirty I was convinced that I'd reversed my real roots, the original ones, which now seemed like a simulacrum. In those woods, years ago, I would get lost, happily, searching for hidden, feverish life in the cool, dark earth. But now that I had moved far away from that world, I never turned over another rock. I knew by then that even Dante, in Purgatory, has to look under boulders. *Ma guarda fiso là, e disviticchia / col viso quel che vien sotto a quei sassi.* I knew that we were the worms.

· 4 ·

You travel a certain distance, you desire and make decisions, and you're left with recollections, some shimmering and some disturbing, that you'd rather not conjure up. But today, in the basilica, memory dominates, the deepest kind. It waits for you under the rock—bits of yourself, still living and restless, that shudder when you expose them.

There's one crossing my mind at this moment, for instance, as we rise and sit, as we pray and listen to the priest who recites the funereal homilies. *Vogliamo essere pronti. Non sappiamo quando verrai a cercarci.* It's a memory buried by a summer, in that stretch of marriage when everything seems to be humming along, on vacation with two other families, ten days, one house on the beach rented together, a pergola, a trail in the forest, sandy path up and down to reach the shore, pretty pine grove, limoncello after dinner, card games, shooting stars, and long conversations until late at night generated by the forced intimacy of the group. We knew the first family only slightly, and we didn't know the second family at all. But our daughter was good friends with the daughter of the first family, who always went on vacation with the second.

The public beach extended for miles, and every morning we'd claim a few umbrellas for ourselves. At lunch we squeezed together at a slanted wooden table sheltered by the pine grove, tired and starved and baked by the sun. Elbows and knees brushed up against one another. The husband of the second couple had studied abroad for a few years. His mother was American, he had green eyes, his grandparents didn't live that far from my parents' town. He understood certain details about my past, my childhood. He knew about this kind of lemon ice that we bought from vans parked along the street in summer, and the long lines to eat boiled lobster with melted butter. He was an anthropologist, hard at work on a book about popular superstitions: owls that were considered bad omens, the live hens newly married women carried over by hand when they made the move from their parents' home to their husband's, along with an odd number of cakes and eggs.

One morning under the umbrellas he and I were left alone to talk about Dante and other things. He was very handsome, tanned, with a compact beard and dark wet hair that glistened, and he spoke to me about his projects with a contagious energy. But I was disoriented by the way he propped his chin in a little cup formed by his hand, and by the expressive fingers of that same hand that would move around all the while as if they were individual letters of a private sign language, grazing his throat, his mouth, ending up now and then under one of the lenses of his glasses. I, meanwhile, because he asked, told him things I'd never mentioned to my husband—nothing terribly secret, just a few of my impressions about how it had been to start a new life in Italy, trivial things, for example, getting used to a washing machine that took three hours to complete a cycle, or getting used to indulging in those long hours in the piazza, after dropping my daughter off at school, just to get some sun or chat with other mothers instead of rushing off to the next appointment. All this he took in without looking at me but with remarkable concentration, his face always partially concealed by his hand, and I remember that when my husband joined us after a long swim he seemed somehow faded in comparison to the other man; he was still good looking, but he didn't have much to say, and his eyes were red and his wet hair was already gray and thinning.

The day following this episode my daughter was brushing her hair on the bed when she said there were tiny dots moving on her pillow. My husband wasn't there, he'd taken the car to go visit a wine cellar and so it was the anthropologist who took me to the nearest pharmacy. Just the two of us in the car, a very hot time of day. Fields full of watermelon. A trip that took twenty minutes, with glimpses of the sea and the beaches from the highway. He told me about the meaning of a passing comet (disaster, always) or an aurora borealis. We'd already noticed the pharmacy the evening before, after dinner, when we were all driving in our separate cars through the town: the owners of the pharmacy had been celebrating their grand opening, with people gathered in the parking lot, balloons and bottles of champagne. I bought shampoo and a comb for lice. And that afternoon, back at the sea, when the others went swimming, I stayed in with my daughter to wash and comb out her hair again and again. We sat in the sun and the lice would emerge, dead or alive, from her straight hair, slipping from her startlingly white scalp—a pallor that made me think of the fish that swim at the very bottom of the ocean or, rather, of underground organisms. My daughter was horrified, but I knew it was another prophetic sign.

In September, after our children returned to school along with all the other kids and teenagers in the city, the anthropologist and I started having lunch in the courtyard of a hotel not far from this church, a hotel with a secluded feel given that it was once a monastery. There's a small university close by, where he was teaching, one class a week. To get to the courtyard of the hotel you had to walk past a chapel and then cross a long hallway with a few paintings scattered on the walls and a checkerboard floor in black and white. We ate unmemorable food among the strung-out tourists. Not far from the hotel there was a museum that was always empty, and we'd go there to walk under the high, frescoed ceilings, through that blissfully indifferent silence, to look at a series of paintings of food—heaps of fruit, gutted fish, glasses of wine—maybe because we were still hungry. Afterward we'd climb up a set of narrow, crooked stone steps. Even though, at first, most of the time we spent together was outside, being with him was like finding yourself in that extra room that mysteriously appears in dreams and makes your house feel surprisingly more spacious. The discovery of that room took me back to a moment in my distant past, when I was afraid to love but also afraid that no one would want me. Until, after Dante Alighieri's letter, I felt suddenly in the wrong, tormented by an impossible situation. Once more, temptation and hesitation on a bench: at the end of the walk we'd sit down and eventually we'd kiss, yes, and look out at the sunset and take in that terrible instant when the city blazes and mountains join the sky and the tops of the umbrella pines rise from the buildings like volcanic smoke and nearly everything that surrounds us day after day, every detail and every living soul, darkens and disfigures and, in a blink, comes to an end.

· 5 ·

The meetings on the bench, which led to afternoons in a room in that hotel with the checkerboard floor, went on for a couple of months. We never spent a night together, but if we fell asleep after sex I would feel that little pool of hair at the small of his back below my hand, and his arm wrapped around me, and if I opened my eyes I'd see, with my addled brain, how his wrist practically disappeared and turned as thin as a skeleton bone. But then we ended it, my father-in-law got sick, he deteriorated rapidly, and it was all about to turn very complicated. It was no time to confess a fleeting affair to my husband (years later I did confess, but only to a few of my girlfriends—women are vaults). I still loved my husband and naturally I felt guilty, incredibly guilty, like a worm, really, but I also felt liberated, I must admit, from the false virtue that had hindered me in the past. Maybe I was afraid to die without ever crossing the line. In any case, every evening at the dinner table with my husband and every night as he snored beside me in bed, I knew that I'd damaged, perhaps ruined, regrettably, the solid relationship we'd had, the same way I'd bend the stalk of a fresh flower at a tragic angle as I adjusted a bouquet just picked out at the flower stand.

If he'd pressed, I probably would have told him everything,

and maybe we would have righted that bent stalk. But he asked nothing, and after my father-in-law died life went on. If we ever talked about that vacation at the sea, and the people we'd had lunch with for ten days in the pine grove, there was never any tension. But I was on edge. I left the coffeepot burning on the stove too many times. One Sunday morning I even caused a small fire to break out in our kitchen, after I'd left a pot holder too close to the burner. And I suspect that my husband—as I apologized to him, as I cried in his arms, as the two of us stood in our pajamas surrounded by that bitter smoke that cuts your throat—had already intuited everything.

Venimmo poi in sul lito diserto. When I was forty years old, and my daughter was sixteen, and my husband was nearly sixty— suffice to say, three different and important ages—I returned to my studies. I wanted to move on, I didn't want to end up a housewife abroad like my mother, forever. Our daughter, who was always clinging to me when she was little, now disappeared, depressed, into her room, and she went out every night, I had no idea whom with. In the place of pigtails she now had a nearly shaved head. My husband had become the director of an important clinic and was always busy. I enrolled at a university outside Rome and commuted there a few times a week. Once more: notebooks, classes, homework. I got my master's, and thanks to that I learned how to teach Dante's language and culture to the rest of the world, at which point I started to work for a society in the center that bears his name. I gave lessons to tourists or foreigners like me, who wanted to read a bit of the *Commedia* in the original or rent a villa with a pool in some pretty town. Once again the poet, the real one, the dead one, paved the way and spurred me on.

One day I got a phone call from my father: my mother had an obstruction in her intestine. I returned hastily to America for the operation—my husband told me it was quite serious—and two weeks later, unable to rally after the surgery, she died in the hospital with her belly swollen as if she were pregnant. In the end I think my mother-in-law knew me better or, at least, had seen the better part of me. But I knew that, in making my bed for as long as she could, and sending a package to Rome every year with a dress that was too big for my daughter, my mother had loved me, too. I stayed on a month to help my father; he was about to retire, he wanted to sell the house, give away furniture and possessions, and move to a small condo. As we emptied the house, he pulled out all my report cards since I was eight years old, along with certificates and essays I'd written, and even my college thesis on the *Commedia;* he'd saved all this in a special box. I searched, in my room, among the things I'd never bothered to throw away, for the love letter I'd received from Dante Alighieri. It had vanished.

And so a new phase of my life began, involving lots of back-and-forth: every two or three months, I'd go visit my retired, widower father. Having lost one parent, I didn't want to miss out on the time I had left with the other. Those trips, grueling as they were, brought me peace. I didn't mind spending two weeks with him, filling his fridge and freezer with food. I observed that when it grew dark in the house he often didn't bother turning the lights on, instead he just sat in his chair without noticing. I took him out for walks, albeit silent, in the woods along the brook with the treetops that look like roots. He never asked me to spend that time with him, he never thanked me aloud for coming, but every time I did I would find, in his small new kitchen, rosy grapefruits among the spotted bananas in the fruit bowl, and a packet of salt and vinegar potato chips, and coffee ice cream.

One time at the airport, at the boarding gate, shortly before the flight, I met a bright young Italian professor. He was sitting next to me and had a tote bag with the name of my college on it. He taught there and told me they were looking for a person who might teach a language course for a year. I applied for the job and got the position. My husband drove me to the airport, we said we'd see each other at Christmas.

I settled into a carriage house, already furnished, behind the huge residence of an important professor. It was a friendly space with reddish wooden floors, a real fireplace I would light in the evenings, and a series of small dormer windows. Just one key, slightly bent, opened the door. Once again I was surrounded by green meadows and tall trees and the sound of power tools that trimmed grass and blew leaves, snow to shovel in the mornings, the creaking of the house when the wind blew, sidewalks built only for strolling, never leading anywhere in particular, that would freeze after snowstorms. It felt odd, returning to a former life, being among those same buildings, those same statues on the campus grounds, the same library where I would earn pocket money as a student, where the same armchair in my favorite corner awaited me.

I enjoyed teaching, the students were smart and asked lots of questions, a few colleagues were kind and invited me to dinner. The second semester I even attended the same Dante course I had taken, decades before, only this time I helped the professor—the young man I'd met in the airport—with correcting the students' exams. The carriage house was cheerful, before me an artist had lived there and had painted pretty designs on the doors and over the fireplace. On Sundays I went to see my father and we walked quietly in the woods along the brook. I often made him a Bundt cake that he liked, using my mother-in-law's recipe. I talked to my husband on the phone every three or four days. He told me what was happening in Rome, if it was sunny or rainy, talked about our friends and family members and about what he was doing. At times, when he called on Sundays from Fregene or Anzio, where he was taking the dog on a long walk, I would wonder who he was with. At the end of the year the college offered me a renewable contract for three years. I could go back to Rome for summers and winters. My husband came to visit me, once, in the carriage house, a brief, melancholy visit during Easter, when the yellowish leaves of the trees had yet to unfold, and the branches' shadows on the grass were still stark and clean. *Poco più oltre, sette alberi d'oro / falsava nel parere il lungo tratto / del mezzo ch'era ancor tra noi e loro.*

He's stayed on in our old apartment, and I've found a smaller one in the same neighborhood. I have a little terrace with succulents and a room for guests, or for my daughter if she comes down from the North. With all the ups and downs, we've stayed married, we've remained friends, and when I go back to Rome, when we both have the time, we might still have lunch together.

· 6 ·

Certain stories are hard to bear, as are certain things we've lived or observed or fumbled or explored with great care.

They transmit an energy that extends beyond the disposable day-to-day. Our deepest memories are like infinite roots reflected in the brook, a simulacrum without end. And yet every story, like every life, lasts only so long. My mother-in-law, for example, passed away with her hair undone, waiting for the nurse to gather it up above her neck, waiting to have a spoonful of the soup they'd prepared for her. *Ma ora, Signore, hanno trovato la pace, la pace che doni loro e che rimane, una serenità che nulla può turbare, una calma imperturbabile.*

· 7 ·

There aren't many people at the funeral, and I'm part of the inner core. I see a few relatives of my husband, a few of his colleagues. I see the women I always chat with at the coffee bar. Some are separated like me, or already widows; a few are still married. Most of us are in our fifties, which means sixty is around the corner. We push two or three small tables together and talk a bit about everything: illnesses and projects and hormones and children, feeling orphaned in middle age, long quiet evenings spent doing nothing, the embarrassment of interrupting our children when they're texting a friend and feeling like an intruder. When I'm in Rome we go out together, we go to the movies or to the theater, we have a drink along the Tiber, or we walk among the crowds, an environment that hosts and hides every transgression on earth. We organize dinners and vacations, hiking expeditions, one week a year we rent a nice house on the beach somewhere. We look up the houses online, we talk about them in our group chat, we wonder who the owners are.

These women in the middle of life's journey are the third family I've had. But we, too, have placed a big collective lid over our wounds, our disappointments, our anguish. Why else would it be that I wake up on two different continents convinced that there's someone in the house, why would I think it's my daughter, still young, running through the rooms or knocking on the door as I take a shower? Or that my husband, an early riser, is still in the kitchen putting on the first pot of coffee and pulling out the jam jars? Distances help, as does changing one's perspective on a regular basis—they make the end of a long marriage easier to bear, they lighten the load of an unhappy childhood and an adolescence spent under a rock and the fear of having ruined nearly everything.

Within a week I'll be in the taxi again, on the Rome–Fiumicino highway, to fly back to the other side. Daytime flight, nine hours. Maybe the exertion does me good. I'll go back to close out the semester and spend hours in the library, where I know where to drape my coat so that it stays toasty over the radiator. My ears will turn cold as soon as I step outside to go home. You can count the colored leaves still attached to the trees one by one. The dry rustle as they fall and strike the windowpanes sounds like rain. At dusk, once in a while, I'll see a rabbit sitting on the grass, its body round and compact and that black marble eye staring out at nothing, or maybe everything. The animal emits terror or else it simply mirrors my own, and I wonder what it would have been like to live without moving so often between places, without the migrating spirit that has befallen me.

Were there people, in Dante's time, condemned to have more than one life—that is, to never have one full life? It's not easy to open the carriage house door with that bent key, when already at five-thirty in the afternoon it's so outrageously dark outside, and to know that no one is inside waiting for you. Every time I squeeze between the front door and the storm door made of metal and glass, I feel a dreadful weight at my shoulders. It's awkward searching for the key while the storm door presses against me, and I wonder if the tired breath the door lets out before closing comes from the stubborn hinges or from me.

I'd call the academic side of this two-sided life a sort of purgatory. Rome switches between heaven and hell. By now it's chock-full of things that have been broken, mistaken, bent, tossed, killed, but I can't cut my ties. It's hard to govern my succulents on the terrace, they don't pardon my comings and goings. Am I giving them too much water or not enough? Why do the leaves of the jade plant fall off as soon as I touch them? My skin turns thin, or else my blood flows differently—in recent years, if I hit my hand against something hard, a pole on the street or a piece of wood, even if I bang my finger against a pan as I'm doing the dishes, I get a small hematoma that hurts like mad, and I feel like the same old idiot who clumsily wrecks and ruins things, who stains brand-new boots and expensive blouses the first time I wear them. And my poor fountain pen, the twisted nib like a hooked nose. Was this the amazing life Dante Alighieri had predicted?

The light no longer enters the basilica, the sun has shifted. *Il cielo non è così lontano, malgrado la nostra impressione di distanza infinita.* I look up again at the divine figure stuck to the ceiling. She seems suspended, about to fall, to plunge facefirst. But she doesn't cede. Only words cede, those spoken and delivered by hand, and friendships, and cells, and shoes with leopard spots and Sunday lunches of long ago, and passions in adolescence and in adulthood, and stores that sell knives and small appliances, parental worries, children's voices, clamshells on the edge of your plate. A few regrets endure. I still wait to be forgiven by my husband, and to say, when I'm seventeen, to a tortured and fearless boy, that I love him, too.

· 8 ·

Today is the first day I realize that I've never told anyone the story of Dante Alighieri. Until today it's nested *in quella parte del libro de la mia memoria*. I still dream about him: he's arrived on foot with a flashlight in his hand, he waits for me on the other side of the storm door, he's come to visit.

· 9 ·

We rise. I see a man sitting alone who's been writing something, totally absorbed, as if the entire church were his study. Behind him, at the back, I see other tourists. They, too, have attended my mother-in-law's funeral. Years ago, before I met my husband at a bus stop, I would have been among them, still awaiting my new life. *Sono più vicini a noi quelli che ci hanno lasciati per un mondo migliore.* It's strange to feel married, in the end, more to a place than to a person. I hope to die here and nowhere else.

They carry away the coffin, we form a line, and we, too, leave the church. I cry for my mother, who knew me too little, while they place my mother-in-law in the hearse. Now she'll be buried next to her husband, below the earth with the insects I used to look for under rocks. The only everlasting lid. *La gente che per li sepolcri giace / potrebbesi veder? già son levati / tutt' i coperchi, e nessun guardia face.* I hug various people. I hug my husband last. I tell him I'm tired, that I didn't sleep well on the plane, and that I won't be able to continue on to the cemetery.

He thanks me for coming.

"We'll miss her."

He replies, sweetly, "She loved you very much."

He's gotten old but not with me. He says goodbye and gives me two kisses before walking toward his car with our neighbor.

HOW LONG must we live to learn how to survive?

How many times *incipit vita nova*?

I make plans to have dinner with my friends. A clear blue sky extends over the piazza.

"This city is shit," one of us says, breaking the silence. "But so damn beautiful."

if you enjoyed
WILDWOOD MAGIC
look out for

WILDWOOD WHISPERS

by

Willa Reece

Mel Smith is heartbroken after the sudden death of her best friend, Sarah Ross. To fulfill a final promise to her, Mel travels to an idyllic small town nestled in the Appalachian Mountains. But Morgan's Gap is more than she ever expected.

There are secrets that call to Mel in a salvaged remedy book filled with the magic of simple mountain traditions and in the connection she feels to the Ross homestead and the wilderness around it.

With every taste of sweet honey and tart blackberries, the wildwood twines further into Mel's broken heart. But a threat lingers in

*the woods—one that may have something to do with Sarah's
untimely death and has now set its sights on Mel.*

*The wildwood is whispering. It has secrets to reveal—if
you're willing to listen....*

Prologue

April 2009

I was prepared.

I was always prepared.

Before recess, I opened my locker and felt the bottom of the Wonder Woman book bag hanging on the hook. The lumps created by several tightly rolled T-shirts, shorts and pairs of underwear made me feel better. In another locker, one hall away from mine, Sarah's book bag was also carefully packed.

I wished I could check it too, even though I already had before we left our foster home that morning.

Recess was never okay. And it was even worse now that I had a "sister" to protect. Bullies seemed to know when you didn't have adult backup. No loving mom or dad who would swoop down and save you if things went south.

I had been saving myself for a long time. Unlike Sarah, I'd been in the system for as long as I could remember. I pulled my hand back from the book bag and slammed the locker door harder than I should have. The bang sounded loud even in a hallway full of students rushing

toward the one free half hour out of the day. I didn't look up. I cringed inside and forced my fists to relax. I laid my palms flat on the cool, dented metal of the closed locker as if I could shush it now. Too late. I'd called attention to myself. It felt like a hundred sets of eyes were on my bowed back.

So, I did what I had to do.

I turned, straightened my spine, and squared my shoulders.

I was already over five feet five inches tall. Bigger than most of the kids in my grade. And on my head was a wild cap of muddy brown curls that added a couple more inches to that. Tall or not, the whole world still considered me just a kid. *I'm ancient only on the inside.* I met the first set of staring eyes I came to and locked on with my best "What are you looking at?" face. The boy looked away. I did that several more times until the whole crowd moved on.

Recess was a daily challenge I faced with the grim determination of a soldier marching onto the battlefield. Before Sarah, I could always find a quiet corner, and my size made me less likely to become a target. Sure, there were rumors about me. Bored people can make up some crazy shit. But teachers talk too and sometimes their voices carry between districts.

I hadn't always known to lay low.

The system didn't like fighters. It had taken me eleven years to learn that. I kept our book bags packed because flight was best. Bugging out instead of hitting back was always the plan. Caseworkers liked that. Runners got extra counseling. Different placements. Sympathy from overwhelmed men and women "just trying to do their jobs." Sarah didn't understand all the tricky stuff yet. She was a year older than me, but inexperienced in spite of what she'd been through.

If you didn't contribute to the blood and bruises, you were much better off.

Sarah Ross had come into the foster care system in Richmond from far away. She spoke like every word was a song and she didn't know anything about bullies or living in the city. She was small and so vulnerable my fists clenched again thinking about it.

She was the first best friend I'd ever had. Only I knew her real last name. To everyone else she was a "Smith" like me.

Three months ago I'd been *Jane* Smith. No name. No family. No hope that anyone would adopt a girl with a record of anger management issues. But Sarah didn't care that I had been born a fighter into an unfair world that made me use my fists and punished me for using them at the same time. Maybe she even liked it a little. My hot anger was the opposite of Sarah's icy grief. Our friendship had been instant. We'd pinky sworn our sisterhood at midnight by the glow of a superhero night-light.

Sarah had given me the name Mel the very next day. And I had run with it, feeling more like a Mel than I ever had a Jane.

"Sarah's trapped at the top of the monkey bars and Jason is posting upskirt shots online," a girl shouted at me as I exited the building and started to look around. Wendy Solomon sounded more pleased than upset. As if recess was much more fun with a little torture and sexual harassment going on.

Most of the students had abandoned whatever they'd been doing to gather in a ring around the monkey bars, where the biggest kid in school, even bigger than me, had cornered Sarah.

Sarah was quiet and peaceful and way too old for playground equipment, but she could never lay low when the sun was high and the playground was open. Something about the outdoors drew her as if every scrubby blade of grass was a miracle. Sarah never seemed to notice the noise of traffic or the pollution haze across the sky. Or the bullies that stalked her because they liked her rounded shoulders and hollow eyes.

I didn't pause. I didn't even consider walking to the other side of

the playground, where an empty bench might help me to stay out of it. I wouldn't leave Sarah to the small huddle of teachers near the basketball court where a weed-clogged fence gave them cover to smoke. Not even when butting in would further wreck my file.

But I didn't run. I walked, as carefully as I could, across the playground. No one paid me much attention. Rumors were one thing. Personal experience another. I'd never scrapped at recess here. I'd avoided bullies and pretended to be chill.

Only Sarah knew better. And right now, only Sarah watched me head in her direction.

I could imagine how it had all gone down. The spring day was warm and clear. Butterflies flitted over the dandelions that poorly paid landscapers hadn't even bothered to poison and kill. Sarah had eagerly run outside while I was dragging my feet. She'd scrambled up to the top of the monkey bars to get even closer to the white cottony clouds she loved to watch.

And Jason Mews had been right behind her.

I should have rushed outside. I should have been there to guard the ladder and protect my friend from pervs.

I was close enough now to see Sarah's red eyes and flushed cheeks. I could see her white-knuckled grip on the rusty metal bars and the sheen of tears on her face. And the hot, hard knot of anger that always wrapped around my insides, squeezing my lungs and holding me back, broke loose and set me free.

I ran.

I ran at Jason and slammed into him with the force and fury of ten thousand times when I'd wanted to but hadn't. He was knocked off his feet and his cell phone flew from his fingers. It fell in the mulch beneath Sarah, and my foot came down on the screen, hard, once, then twice, while Jason caught his breath.

"Mel," Sarah said. Her voice trembled, but it sounded hopeful and relieved.

I needed to warn her that this wasn't going to end well. The system didn't favor heroes. Victims were better, quieter, more easily managed. But, before I could put the complicated lesson into words, Jason swung out a long leg and kicked me off my feet. I went down with a thud into the mulch that was so thinly spread hard-packed earth showed in a bunch of places.

My chin found one of the bare spots and pain exploded in bright flashes behind my eyes. I tasted blood and gasped its sickly metallic flavor down my throat. I hated that taste. I always hated it. The taste of blood was usually followed by worse things.

"What? You the only one that can peek at the hillbilly's pink lace, Ankle Bracelet?" Jason asked.

I'd never had to wear a juvenile court monitor, but rumors had inspired the nickname and I hadn't bothered to deny it. Maybe, in the back of my mind, I'd figured it would be true, sooner or later. Laying low was hard.

I gagged and spit blood into the dirt. Kids were yelling now. Some encouraged Jason to kick me again. Their shouts somehow hurt me more than the fall had. Others warned the teachers were coming. I ignored them. I also ignored the pain. I grabbed two fistfuls of mulch and pushed myself up on my knees.

"Stay down, Ankle Bracelet," Jason warned, then he turned away from me to clown with his friends as if he was already sure I would listen.

Sarah and I were only foster kids. And no one was going to save us.

Staying down would have been the right thing to do. Oops. I fell. Just an accident. No reason for a teacher to get involved. So far, I'd only shoved a much bigger kid. Stomped his phone. Big deal. There

was no blood *on him*. No bruises. Me being the bloody one might actually work in my favor. The problem was he deserved so much more. Especially when I glanced back at him and saw him still looking up Sarah's dress.

I ignored his warning. My jaw ached, but I struggled back to my feet. Handfuls of mulch made my fists bigger.

The problem with lying low was that bullies like Jason deserved to bleed.

"They're pink, guys. And the elastic is torn and hanging out on one leg," Jason said, then he laughed. Because poor kids were funny. Because if he didn't mock and laugh and hurt someone else bad stuff might happen to him too. He was cruel because if he was kind he might feel our pain. Some of his friends in the crowd laughed and shouted nasty suggestions, but others got really quiet because they had seen me stand.

The first teacher was pushing her way through the students who had ringed the scene when Jason turned back toward me, warned something was up by stares and gestures. I didn't hesitate. This chance couldn't be lost. He was bigger, but I was madder. I put all my weight behind the swing. Blood flew from Jason's busted lip as my knuckles connected with his smirking face. His body spun halfway around before he fell, hard, knocked off his feet. Mulch scattered in a satisfying spray as he came to a rest. Stunned. The whole playground was stunned. Except for Sarah, who had seen the blow coming from a hundred yards away.

The momentum of my swing carried me forward and into the teacher's arms as she burst through the crowd to join us under the monkey bars. The look on Ms. Tatum's face pretty much confirmed my philosophy about lying low, but I focused on Sarah instead. My best friend. My sister. Family. She looked down at me from her perch with the first huge grin I'd ever seen on her face. The smile made her

seem less pale. Like okay could be possible if we held on to each other. Jason howled curses from the ground at my feet. Ms. Tatum's hands closed cruelly around my upper arms. But our bug-out backpacks waited in our lockers and Sarah was smiling.

I'd always been a fighter.

But I hadn't always known family was worth fighting for.

April 2019

Mel didn't wear perfume. She didn't have to. Even though her chestnut curls were always kept back with strong clips and a perky visor with the coffee chain's logo on it, the scent of coffee permeated her hair and skin and clothes. No wonder. She worked, constantly, picking up extra shifts and volunteering for overtime and inventory because nursing school wasn't cheap. Sarah had always wanted to be a nurse.

Nearly always.

She could remember a time when she'd dreamed a different sort of dream. Growing up in the western Virginia mountains with her herbalist mother, she'd always assumed she would be a healer. She shied away from thinking about why that goal had morphed into another, with Mel's help.

Sarah breathed deeply of Mel's comforting coffee scent.

She could never go home again. At least not while she was living. It wasn't safe. One day, she would be buried there. With her mother. Until then, she would learn to heal in more modern ways.

The fragrance of Mel's job filled the apartment that morning as she drank the cup of herbal tea Sarah had made her. Beside her cup, nothing but crumbs were left of the toast Sarah had also made, but she knew better than to try to make her eat more. Mel's budget

consciousness begrudged every piece of her own toast consumption while usually urging Sarah to eat more than her share.

Never had an actual sister worried over a sibling the way Mel worried over Sarah. At first, it had been a relief to accept Mel's caretaking. When the loss of her mother had been sharp and fresh. When the new sights and sounds and expectations in the city were so different from the hushed world of the whispering woods where she'd grown up.

Mel had pushed back, literally, against the bullies who would mock Sarah's accent or her backwoods ways. Against the people who would have preyed on her because she didn't know anything about surviving as an orphan and she'd been so slammed by loss she'd been too slow to learn. She'd come to the Richmond Children's Home completely wrecked by the ruin of the only life she'd ever known.

And Mel had caught her as she was falling, before she could hit the ground.

Never mind that Mel, as an unplaceable foster kid, had her own problems. She had taken Sarah under her wing and taken care of everything from that moment on. And Sarah had let her. Until now. After six months of nursing school, Sarah realized that Mel wasn't going to sign up for classes too, like she'd promised. She wasn't going to stop making do with less food, less clothing, less of everything, so that Sarah could have more.

Not unless Sarah forced her to.

A daunting thought. No one forced Mel to do anything she didn't want to do. She was ever and always immovable. Like the sun...or maybe more like the moon. Definitely more night than day. Sarah brought the warmth to the tiny family they'd made. With tea and crotchet. With houseplants and silly texts to try to make Mel smile. Mel brought the predictable power of the tides. She propelled their

lives, but always for Sarah, never for herself. Only Sarah knew that there was more to Mel, beneath the work and worry.

"You need more time away from the coffee shop," Sarah said. Mel's eyelids drooped with exhaustion, but her mouth still managed to smirk at the very idea of rest.

"I'll sleep all afternoon. I promise," Mel said. She'd tossed the hated visor on the table beside her plate and now she pulled the clips from her hair. They often caused her to have headaches. She pushed her hands into her hair to massage her scalp, probably dealing silently with one now rather than complain about it.

But Sarah often knew things others didn't know.

For instance, she knew that Mel wasn't meant to brew coffee for the rest of her days. She just didn't know how to make her shift her focus from caretaker to taking care of herself.

"They'll call you in early. And you'll go because I won't be here to stop you," Sarah said. Mel shrugged and sipped some more tea, not bothering to deny it.

She wanted to tell Mel that trouble was brewing. Beyond Mel's workaholic ways, there was something else nibbling at the edges of Sarah's senses. A warning. She heard it in the call of the doves on the ledges outside their apartment windows. She heard it in the wind whistling through the trees on the street. There was still some nature in her life and Sarah couldn't ignore what it was trying to say. But she wasn't sure how to convey this knowing to Mel without adding to the already heavy burdens she was determined to carry on her strong shoulders.

Her sister in every way but blood stood up and drained the rest of the tea from her cup. She placed it back on the table with a decisive clunk. But she did pause beside Sarah's chair and lean to kiss the top of her head.

"Get to class. I've got this," Mel said, bumping her hip against Sarah's side. It didn't negate the affectionate kiss. But it did punctuate the end of their conversation.

Sarah watched Mel retreat from serious conversation to her room. Where, in spite of the valerian tea, she would probably toss and turn over how to pay for Sarah's residency scrubs and how long she could ignore the fact that she needed new shoes. When Mel's bedroom door closed, Sarah reluctantly reached for the "For Fox Sake" cup she'd saved pennies to buy for Mel last Christmas. She needed to see the dregs of the ground valerian root in the bottom of the cup, although she dreaded what they would say.

Her heart pounded and her eyes went wide. The lumps and swirls in the bottom of Mel's cup negated the fox's cartoon smile. Sarah dropped the cup to the table. It clattered over onto its side. She glanced toward Mel's bedroom door and halfway rose to go to her—for comfort? To warn her? It was no use to try either. Her glance moved to the apartment door down the hall and froze there. The three extra dead bolts Mel had installed weren't going to protect them forever. The danger that had driven Sarah from the mountain still stalked her, and even Mel wouldn't be able to catch her when she fell this time.

And who would catch Mel?

Sarah gathered up the breakfast dishes quietly and washed the dregs down the sink, hoping she was wrong. While she cleaned, she strained her ears for answers, but the cooing doves outside the window had nothing more to say.

THE LOWLAND

Born just fifteen months apart, Subhash and Udayan Mitra are inseparable brothers, one often mistaken for the other in the Calcutta neighborhood where they grow up. But they are also opposites, with gravely different futures ahead. It is the 1960s, and Udayan—charismatic and impulsive—finds himself drawn to the Naxalite movement, a rebellion waged to eradicate inequity and poverty; he will give everything, risk all, for what he believes. Subhash, the dutiful son, does not share his brother's political passion; he leaves home to pursue a life of scientific research in a quiet, coastal corner of America. But when Subhash learns what happened to his brother in the lowland outside their family's home, he goes back to India, hoping to pick up the pieces of a shattered family, and to heal the wounds Udayan left behind—including those seared in the heart of his brother's wife. Masterly suspenseful, sweeping, and piercingly intimate, *The Lowland* is a work of great beauty and complex emotion: an engrossing family saga and a story steeped in history that spans generations and geographies with seamless authenticity. It is Jhumpa Lahiri at the height of her considerable powers.

Fiction

ALSO AVAILABLE

The Clothing of Books
In Other Words
Unaccustomed Earth
Whereabouts

A NOTE ABOUT THE TRANSLATOR

Todd Portnowitz is the translator of *Long Live Latin: The Pleasures of a Useless Language,* by Nicola Gardini; *The Greatest Invention: A History of the World in Nine Mysterious Scripts,* by Silvia Ferrara; *In Search of Amrit Kaur: A Lost Princess and Her Vanished World,* by Livia Manera Sambuy; and *Go Tell It to the Emperor: The Selected Poems of Pierluigi Cappello.* He is the recipient of a Raiziss/de Palchi Fellowship from the Academy of American Poets. He lives in Brooklyn, New York.

Acknowledgments

Several stories originally appeared in the following publications: "The Boundary" in *The New Yorker,* January 29, 2018, and as "Il confine" in *Granta Italia* (2015); "The Reentry" ("La riunione") as "Pranzo avariato" in *La Lettura–Corriere della Sera* (2018); "P's Parties" ("Le Feste di P.") as "La festa di P." in *Nuovi Argomenti* 1 (May–August 2019), and in *The New Yorker* (July 10 & 17, 2023); "The Delivery" in *A Public Space,* No. 29 (January 2021), and as "Il ritiro" in *Nuovi Argomenti* 5 (September–December 2020); "Well-Lit House" as "Casa luminosa" in *Nuovo Decameron* (HarperCollins Italia, 2021); and "Notes" as "I bigliettini" in *Le ferite: quattordici grandi racconti per i cinquant'anni di Medici Senza Frontiere* (Einaudi, Turin, 2021).

"P's Parties," "Well-Lit House," and "Notes" were translated by Todd Portnowitz; the remaining stories in this book were self-translated by the author.